THE FREEDOM STONE

THE FREEDOM STONE

by Judi Howe

ShayMark Press

www.JudiHowe.com

ISBN# 978-0-9994302-7-9

Book design: Diana Wade

ShayMark Press

Cornelius, North Carolina

Praise for *The Freedom Stone*

If we don't understand and learn from history, we will not understand when history is being repeated. *The Freedom Stone* presents an accurate historical detail of what the experience was like, both on the plantation, and on the path to freedom. This valuable work invites middle-grade readers to put themselves in the shoes of Moses and Addie, two runaway slaves seeking to escape the atrocities of slavery and flee to the North. More importantly, this book will be a useful tool in the classroom for educators who wish to go beyond the all-too-often laundered version of American history.

–Howard N. Lee, Founder and President of the Howard N. Lee Institute for Equity and Opportunity in Education

Judi Howe has written a poignant, page-turning story woven through with vital history – about plantation life, slavery, abolitionists, the Underground Railroad, Nat Turner's Rebellion, The Middle Passage and more. I wish I'd had *The Freedom Stone* to read when I was a child.

–Pam Kelley, Author, Money Rock: A Family's Story of Cocaine, Race, and Ambition in the New South

We're all afraid sometimes.
I'm afraid right now, too.
Bravery is doing what you have to do
Even when you are terribly afraid.

-Missus

Slave Households on the Porter Plantation

Cabin 1:

Paris ....old slave, gardener, animal tender
Mabry...........field slave
     Moses - 12 yrs old, gardener, animal tender, helper in the Big House
Lafayette.......field slave
Lizzie ....field slave
     Rachael - baby

Cabin 2:

Cuffy.............carpenter
George..........blacksmith
Susie..............field slave
     Lewis - 15 yrs old, field slave
     Peter - 14 yrs old, field slave
     Elijah - 11 yrs old, field slave
Henry ....field slave
Lavinia..........old slave, child caretaker, cook

Cabin 3:

Barsheeba.....field slave
     Emma - 15 yrs old, field slave
     Delia - 13 yrs old, field slave
     Mingo - 12 yrs old, field slave
Reddick........field slave
Robert ....16 yrs old, field slave

Cabin 4:

Exeter ....field slave
Hanson..........field slave
Flemming.....field slave
Ned ....field slave
Lea ....field slave
     Patsey - 4 yrs old
     Tempie - 1 yr old
Israel.............field slave

CHAPTER ONE

The Porter Plantation
August 1850

Moses

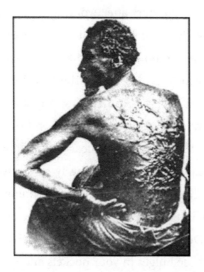

Ben cracked his whip across Paris' back. Not once. Not twice. Over and over again. Each strike tore his shirt and ripped through his skin. Seeing all that blood, running down his back all the way to his waist, made me feel sick. My eyes filled with tears, but I didn't allow them to run down my face.

Paris was whipped more times than I can remember. I was

only eleven years old then, frightened. I could not bear it; it was so hard to watch my friend being punished so severely. For four tomatoes and six carrots. Such a small thing, when the Massa had a whole field full of vegetables. It made me want to yell at Ben, "Stop, please stop!" But I was too afraid. I dared not say a word, or more of us would have to endure the same punishment.

It was a beautiful, crisp day, and Paris and I were on our way back to the slave quarters after working in the vegetable fields all day. Out of the clear blue, behind us, we heard the sound of horse's hooves coming closer and closer. There was Massa, proud as a peacock, on his horse, Thunder. He was looking as mean as I'd ever seen him. And, that's saying something, because he always stomped around with a scowl on his face and an evil eye. It was never a surprise to hear him yelling or shrieking something mean or vulgar. Right away he started hollering at Paris. "Old man, what do you think you're doing, stealing from me? You *work* in these fields; you do not *take* anything. This is *my* property. Do you take me for an imbecile? Did you think I wouldn't see those bulges in your pockets and those carrot-tops sticking out?" Jumping down from his horse, Massa marched right up to Paris and grabbed those carrots. When he went after the tomatoes, he was so rough that he smashed them, getting tomato juice and seeds all over himself. It was all I could do not to laugh. But I knew better.

"You two thieves stand right where you are. If you move even so much as a muscle, I will make it even more difficult for you.

Stealing my property," he muttered under his breath as he rode off to get Ben. *I get so tired of him talking about his property. I'm his property. He owns me the same way he owns those vegetables. Just doesn't seem right that one person can actually own another person.* Of course, he called on Ben, his nasty overseer, to do the dirty work of whipping Paris. Massa didn't want to do it himself, so, when Ben showed up, Massa was nowhere around. I guess he figured that if he didn't see it, it didn't even happen.

I felt guilty because I had some carrots stuffed in my pocket too. I started to say something, but Paris looked me straight in the eye with a stern look on his face. He shook his head "no". I kept my mouth shut.

It took seven or eight days for the bloody gashes on his back to scab over. He couldn't wear a shirt because it stuck to the open sores. Every place where the whip had scored Paris' body was swollen and tender, from his shoulders to his hips, and there was some clear fluid oozing out. When I tried to clean his wounds with vinegar and boiled water, he cried out. It must have hurt bad.

The scores on Paris' back and neck became hard, raised and knotted, giving his back the appearance of Mama's washboard. In my mind, I can still hear Paris' wailing, "Peace, be with me - now!" In his powerful, but sad voice, he sobbed that same phrase over and over again.

Paris was my friend and the oldest slave on the plantation. I don't really know how old Paris was. I just know that he looked old to me then, older than Mama and Papa. Paris and Papa were

5

good friends, but they were quite different. Papa was quiet. He didn't talk much, but when he did, everyone paid close attention. Papa had a calming way of speaking. He spoke so softly that you had to lean in to hear him. I was kind of like Papa. I was always thinking, thinking, thinking. Not very talkative. Paris was not at all tight-lipped like my Papa and me. Land sakes, Paris was a different story. He loved to talk; he could talk your arm right off.

Paris and I shared responsibility for the large gardens of fruits and vegetables that fed the Massa's family. We also cared for the horses and mules that were used in the fields and for pulling the carriages. Massa also had a few cows, for milk, cheese, and for meat. There were many more pigs than cows. Paris explained that pigs were easier and cheaper to raise than cows; pork was easier than beef to smoke and store in the smokehouse, and their manure made good fertilizer for the fields. Massa owned lots of chickens too.

Paris thought of Papa and me as his family, and, in a way, we were. He did not have any family in the slave quarters, and he shared a one-room cabin along with me, Papa, Lafayette and Lizzie, and their baby Rachel. Our wood cabin was often cold and drafty, sometimes wet from driving rains. There were two holes in the ceiling. We tried over and over again to patch them by nailing small pieces of wood over the holes, but it never lasted very long. As soon as a big thunderstorm came up, the rain would pour through the holes. One hole was right over my bed. More than once, Papa and I were awakened in the middle of the night to rain falling on our heads. We'd run out into the yard and grab some big clay pots to put under the holes to catch the water. By then, of course, our bed was sopping wet.

We stuffed moss and straw into the gaps in the whitewashed wood-slatted wall to keep out the wind, but if the winds were really strong, the water and wind would come through the cracks. One night there was an enormous thunderstorm. The lightning and thunder were frightening enough, but when the wind blew through the walls, the moss and straw came flying out of the cracks, blowing all over the cabin. In the morning, Papa took one look at me and burst out laughing. "Moses, I wish you could have a look at yourself! You got moss stuck in your ears and straw sticking out of every hair on your head." I loved seeing Papa laugh. It didn't happen often; he was so serious.

There were two openings that we called windows, one in the front and one in the back, that could be covered with the wooden shutters that hung on the outside. In the summer, the cabin was hot because we had to use the open fireplace that was on the back wall for cooking and to keep the bugs away. Sometimes we cooked outside in the fire pit that was in the center of the slave yard. But then, the mosquitos ate us alive inside the cabin. So, we always had to make a choice - too hot, or too buggy.

Our beds were not really beds. They were nothing more than a pile of straw covered with cloth atop some creaky wooden pallets, but it was a little better than sleeping on the bare floor. I never got used to the sound of mice and rats scurrying about under the pallets during the night.

We never knew when Massa would show up to check on us. Some days he'd march through the fields like a king surveying his kingdom. Other days, he'd stand in a corner of the barn, leaning on one of the horse stalls, and he would stare and stare at Paris and me as if he thought he could catch us doing something, anything, that he didn't like. When we got through a day without seeing the Massa, we thought it was a pretty good day.

"Moses, get over here right this minute!" I was just finishing mucking out the horse stalls, when Massa appeared in the enormous entrance to the barn. Paris and I had flung wide the tall double doors to let the sun and fresh air into that stinky barn. Standing there in that large space, with the sun at his back, Massa looked like a giant. *Oh, oh,* I thought. *This can't be good. I guess I'm in for it.* I had no idea what Massa might have wanted with me. *How can I be in trouble when I am doing exactly what I am supposed to be doing?*

In a split second, I dropped the pitchfork I was using and ran over to the Massa. "Yes, sir?" The words had barely passed my lips when Massa hollered, "Moses, what do you know about this?" He was holding a book in his hand, shaking it at me, as if he might throw it. I couldn't imagine why he might think I would know anything about a book. Slaves weren't even allowed to learn to read. It didn't matter if we told the truth or lied, Massa never believed a word any of us slaves said. So, I had to make a quick decision. *Think! Think fast, Moses.* I told myself. *Better come up with somethin' good.* Then I remembered what Papa always told me, "Tell the truth, son."

"Massa, I don't know anythin' about that book, sir," I answered.

"Of course, you do, you lazy varmint! I found this right here in the barn, over there near the ladder to the hay loft. Someone must be teaching you to read! You better tell me the truth, or I will have Ben take care of you."

I knew what that meant. In my head, I could hear Paris wailing each time the whip slashed across his back. *Don't call for Ben, Massa....please! I didn't steal that book. I'm telling you the truth, Massa.*

"Sir, I am tellin' you the truth. I don't know anythin' about that book."

Grabbing me by my shirt collar, Massa almost ran to the Big House, dragging me along. I was halfway tipped over as he pulled me forward, and my feet were double-timing and scraping the dirt. When we reached the house, I was completely out of breath.

"You stay right here, you good-for-nothing! Massa left me standing outside the door to the Big House as he stomped inside. Mama and my sister Addie worked in the Big House, but I wasn't allowed inside because I was always dirty from working outdoors.

I wanted to sit on the stoop while I waited, but I figured that was probably not a good idea. He'd already called me lazy and good-for-nothin'. *Who knows what he would say if he came back and I was sitting down?* It seemed like forever before Massa came back outside. With him was James, Massa's son and my friend. Standing behind his father, James flashed me one of those big grins of his, and with a little wink that his father didn't see, he said, "Father, don't blame Moses. That book is mine. I'm glad you found it. I was worried that I had lost it. I must have left it in the barn the other day when I was waiting for Moses to finish his work, so we could go fishing."

To me, he said, "Moses, I am so sorry that you got in trouble for something that you had nothing to do with."

Massa must not have known what to say. He grabbed my shirt again, and with a big shove, he threw me to the ground, saying, "Get out of my sight, nigger. I'm done with you for today!"

Massa was an angry, unsettled soul. He always wore a grimace on his face, spoke harshly, and was never happy with anything anyone did. He was hungry for more: more slaves, more land, that he could fill with more tobacco plants. He wanted better clothing, stylish furniture, and fancy dishes. He wanted his neighbor, Frederick Adams, to know that the 450-acre Porter Plantation was bigger and better.

Massa did not want a reputation of being shamelessly hard-hearted and cruel to his slaves. That's what he paid his overseer, Ben, to do. But that didn't stop him from beating his own family. Sometimes, I heard Massa thrashing Missus, or James, or even little Sarah. It usually happened when he had too much to drink. His temper got the best of him then. What a temper! Never knew anybody with such a beastly temper.

I told Massa the truth that day when he thought James' book was mine. If James had not convinced him otherwise, I would have been beaten badly - maybe worse than Paris. There was no way Massa would allow any of his slaves to read. The thought of that would have scared and angered him so much, he might have even killed me.

Chapter Two

Life in the Big House
March 1851

Addie

Most every morning Mama had to fuss at me to get up out of bed. Plain and simple, I loved to sleep. Perhaps sleep was an escape from all the nastiness going on around us… yelling and whipping. Sleep was an escape from the long, hot days cooking over the fire. I was always tired. I needed my sleep.

"Adeline, wake up girl! Gotta be gettin' down to that kitchen and get some fire goin' for the Missus' breakfast," Mama said as she nudged me from my slumber.

"Mama, I don't wanna!" I muttered under my breath.

"No choice about it, Adeline. We have our jobs to do."

I knew better, but I complained anyway, "I don't understand why James and Sarah don't have work to do. Don't seem right."

"Adeline, you just keep that thought to yourself. None of our business what they do. Don't ever let anybody hear you talk like that, hear?"

"Yes, Mama." I quietly agreed, just as I always did. A lot of troubling and gloomy thoughts raced through my mind almost all of the time. I was nervous and I usually got a stomach ache when I worried about how Massa would react to something. *Am I going to do something wrong today that will make Massa angry? What if I make a mistake when I cut the fabric for Missus' new dress? Will I have to live like this the rest of my life?* I learned to nod and to put a small make-believe smile on my face. Just got along better that way.

Mama and I were house slaves, so we lived in a small room in the attic of the Big House. Mama always told me, "You take the good with the bad. In the summer, it is mighty hot up there, but, in the winter, it is a lot warmer than that drafty ol' cabin where Moses and your Papa stay."

Mama tended to everything on the plantation that had to do with Missus Martha and James, 15, three years older than Moses, and Sarah,10, four years younger than I. Mama's jobs included cooking, cleaning, washing the family's clothes, ironing, and slaughtering chickens. I helped Mama and I sewed the clothes for the Massa's family.

It was hard to figure Mama out. Mostly she stayed all clammed-up. Occasionally though she would let out a big ol' hearty laugh or burst out in song like she was standing on some big stage somewhere. Mama had a way of making others feel comfortable. She seemed to know, without a word being said, just when someone needed a hug, either because they were happy or because they were sad. And they were powerhouse hugs too.

Sewing was a peaceful activity for me; I loved seeing the results of my work when Missus or Sarah wore one of the dresses I had sewn for them. Every sewing project had to be perfect. If it wasn't, I kept at it until every stitch was as perfect as the cornrows Mama made on my head. I was particular about my own appearance, always smoothing my skirt and apron, or tucking a stray wisp of hair behind my ear. So, if I was careful about how I looked, why wouldn't I want Missus and Sarah to look perfectly beautiful in the garments I sewed for them?

Mama and I learned that the best way to stay out of Massa's way was to keep quiet. Speak only when spoken to. We said nothing whenever we saw Massa scold Missus over any tiny little thing. One morning after breakfast, Missus told Massa that she needed to go into Culpeper to buy some fabric for a new dress. A simple request. But Massa answered her with a holler. "That will have to wait, Martha! I cannot spare a horse or a wagon for such a silly thing." I wondered, *"Why would he get so mad over that?"* I said nothing.

We said nothing when he hollered at Ben - raked him over the coals - for not getting more hours of work from the field slaves.

We endured endless arguments with James about what was or was not 'fair.'

And we stuck it out when Massa jumped on us about the toast being too brown or not brown enough or if the porridge was too hot, or not hot enough.

Massa bought my mother, Rebecca, at a slave market in Richmond, Virginia in 1833. Her clear, chocolate skin; her lively, almost black eyes, and her tiny delicate stature made her stand out in the group of females being sold on the auction block that day. He knew that purchasing a pretty woman would be a good decision, because his male slaves would likely be interested in her. "Slave marriages are good business," he used to say. "More babies, more slaves." Owning more slaves than another tobacco plantation owner was one measure of success, and Massa wanted nothing more than showing off how successful he was.

It was true that the young men on the plantation were indeed attracted to my mother when she arrived. Papa loved to tell Moses and me the stories about how all of the men in the quarters hoped to make Mama their wife. My parents were married under the draping branches of the enormous black walnut tree that used to sit just behind the four slave cabins on Mill Creek.

Lafayette, the one everyone seemed to think was our preacher, asked my father, "Mabry, do you want this woman?"

And, to my mother, he asked, "Rebecca, do you want this boy?"

After both answered, "Yes," Lavinia, the oldest female slave on the plantation, delivered the straw broom to Lafayette, who laid it on the ground and instructed Mama and Papa to hold hands and to jump over it. When they did, Lafayette announced to Papa, "That's your wife."

For me, every morning started out exactly the same; I ran outside to the woodshed to bring in sticks and firewood to start the fire for cooking in the enormous fireplace in the kitchen. Mama gathered eggs from the chicken coop out near the barn. She told me that if her timing was good, Mama got a quick chance to greet Paris and Moses with a cheery "Mornin'!" Moses usually got an affectionate, motherly hug too.

In the winter, when it was frigid and sometimes snowy, I had to make numerous trips back and forth from the woodshed to the Big House, so there would be enough wood for fires in all of the fireplaces. On those mornings, Mama had to make breakfast without my help, because it took me so long to get fires going in the kitchen, the parlor, the dining room, and the upstairs bedrooms. These fires kept the house toasty warm on biting days.

But that particular day in May was bright and cheerful, so one trip would do it for me.

Massa, Missus, James and Sarah took their places in the fancy and frilly dining room at the front of the house, where the view of the walnut and pecan trees was grand. Massa put his big, round behind on the great armchair at one end of the ornate table, and Missus quietly settled into the gracious chair at the opposite end. James and Sarah, chattering happily together, deposited themselves on either side.

"How are your numbers coming along, Sarah?" Massa inquired. I noticed that he asked the question without even looking at Sarah, and it seemed like his mind was miles away. I couldn't tell if he even really wanted to know, or if he thought he was making polite conversation.

Sarah didn't look at him either. "Just fine, Father. Mother is a good teacher," she answered solemnly, tilting her head forward and closing her eyes.

Sarah was so pretty like Missus; her long dark brown hair set off her fair face. But it often seemed like she was unhappy. Whenever Massa was around, she didn't smile much and she sure didn't talk much. Guess she had decided that she got along better that way, just like me. Sarah was a lot more fun when Massa was nowhere to be seen.

"James, tell Paris to hitch Thunder to the pony cart. I want you to drive into Culpeper to pick up some dishes and glassware that I ordered from England. I got a telegram that they have arrived. You can get the rations from Henry's general store while you're there too," Massa added.

"Happy to do it, Father. May I take Moses along with me?"

Shooting one of his looks at James, Massa growled, "No, you certainly may not! Moses has work to do!"

Massa had an ugly way with those looks of his. He could make his forehead scrunch up and his eyes all mean and scary-looking. When he threw one of those looks your way, you knew you were in for some trouble, even if you had no idea why.

I guess Massa thought he knew most everything, and everybody else had just better agree with him. We all got pretty good at pretending that we agreed with whatever Massa said; even

Missus and Sarah had their ways. They always nodded quietly and murmured, "Yes, sir."

"But, Father, he's just a boy, barely two years older than Sarah. Surely, he doesn't need to work that hard," James ventured. Already taller and bigger than his father, James was not afraid to say what he thought, especially if he felt that somebody was being treated unfairly. Inside my head, I pleaded with James. *"Please, James, let it go this time. Do what Sarah and your Mama do. Keep your thoughts to yourself. He's not going to like what you have to say. Please, James!"*

"Don't you ever question me, James! I will not hear it! Moses is *not* like you and me. And he is *not* just a boy; he is my slave! Moses and all of my twenty-eight slaves are here to work this plantation and to work it hard so that we can sell our tobacco at a high price. The Porter Plantation will take second place to none in this county, I tell you. Our home is like an English estate compared to Frederick Adams' plain farmhouse. And you are quite used to the luxury this plantation gives you! Am I understood?"

James did not say, "Yes, sir." He just nodded his head, but I thought I saw anger in his eyes. Massa must have seen it too, because he got hopping mad.

"James, did you hear me? Do you understand what I said? I can't be letting these slaves think they are on holiday here! They are mine, I repeat *mine*, and I say they must work and work hard. And, if they don't work hard enough, Ben Harrison will see to it that they do. He has his ways, you know; he's as mean as a snake.

Now, answer me James, do you understand?"

"Yes, Father, I understand," muttered James, his head lowered and his eyes focusing on the napkin in his lap, not on his Father. "I am happy to drive Thunder into town."

Mama and I continued to serve breakfast. Then we stood quietly off to the side near the window, trying our best not to get in the middle of it.

Mama and I always listened and learned. We never said anything, just quietly went about our business with a fake sweet look on our faces, not happy, just pleasant and sweet. We learned how to master that phony expression. Couldn't let the Massa think for one minute that we weren't perfectly content being a slave on The Porter Plantation. Mama and I learned a lot this way. Smiling and listening.

It seemed Massa didn't even think we had ears to hear with or brains to comprehend the gist of everything he said. He just talked away, as if Mama and I were not even in the room. I guess he didn't really even think of us as real live people. We were simply his property, just like the horses or mules.

Missus Martha, always trying to keep the peace at the dining table, smiled kindly at Mama when she put those warm, mouth-watering biscuits in front of her. "Your biscuits are so delicious, Rebecca. What is your secret?" asked Missus quietly.

Mama just smiled a little smile and nodded her head ever so slightly. But she said nothing.

But that ol' Massa, he just had to say something! "Martha,

21

don't go saying things like that to Rebecca. She's our slave! It's her job to make good biscuits. When will I make you understand?"

Rising up out his big, hand-carved chair, Massa stomped down to the other end of the table, grabbed Missus' pretty face by her chin, lifting it up so she would have to look right into his ugly face, and slapped her hard, not once but twice! Missus whimpered slightly, but then just lowered her head, just like Sarah always did, trying to avoid any more trouble. I wanted to run to Missus and put my arms around her. I felt so sorry for her. She was such a nice lady. *How could he treat her like that?*

Passing by James as he stormed out of the room, Massa gave James' hair a big pull…hard enough that James jumped up out of his chair, as if he were going to get back at his father.

Better sit back down, I thought.

Better not rile up your father any more.

I wanted to get sassy sometimes and blurt out just exactly what was going around and around in my head. This was one of those times. I knew that James wanted to get smart-mouthed at his father that day too, but he knew as I did that usually it was better to keep your mouth shut. Maybe we learned that from Sarah and Missus.

Enough.

Say nothing more.

It'd just get worse.

Massa stomped off to his study. I didn't know what he studied in there; the door was always closed and I wasn't allowed in there even to clean or to build a fire in the winter.

Missus, James and Sarah finally got to finish their breakfast in peace and quiet.

Somehow, even living with that angry man, Missus Martha Porter was still able to put a smile on her pretty face. She talked softly and gently, and she gave big hugs to James, Sarah, Moses, and me. Sometimes I saw her give an affectionate embrace to Mama too.

After breakfast, Missus called Mama and me into the dining room, "Rebecca, your biscuits are so tasty. I don't care what William says, you should be proud of them. Today would be a great day for you to make some of your delicious strawberry pies. That would be a fitting dessert for our dinner tonight, don't you agree? And, Rebecca, make an extra one for your family, too."

"Yes'm," Mama smiled cautiously, as she studied the bruise beginning to show on Missus' face.

Without even asking for permission, I ran outside to the ice pit, pushed back the heavy lid, and stepped down into the shallow cave-like hole. Grabbing the ice pick stored there, I chipped off a small piece of ice, and ran back to the house and gave it to Missus. She gave me a big hug as she wrapped the ice in her napkin and placed it on her face.

I'm scared.

If Massa gets so mad at Missus that he jumps up out of his chair just so he can hit her, what does he do to her when I can't see them? Will he do that to me?

CHAPTER THREE

Finding a Treasure
May 1851

Moses

B en blew that dreadful, ear-splitting horn before daybreak every morning, with the exception of Sunday. And every morning Rachel, Lafayette and Lizzie's baby, was so frightened by that terrifying blast, that she began bawling to beat the band, her wailing almost as terrible as that booming horn.

Once that horn hit our ears, all of us in our one-room cabin had only a few minutes before we had to be out in the fields at work or we would have to answer to Ben, the overseer.

"I'm way too tired to get up out of this thing that Massa calls a 'bed' before the sun's even up," Papa used to whisper to me as we tried to get ready for the day.

Sharing few words, field slaves Lafayette and Lizzie, Paris, Papa and I ate the same breakfast every day: cold bacon and corn grits. I guess it filled us up, but it was boring.

Once Lizzie calmed baby Rachel down after her reaction to the deafening horn, she sat happily on my lap while we ate. I loved her; she was such a happy baby with a big ol' smile on her face. When I tickled her, her contagious giggle soon had all of us in the cabin giggling with her; that made her giggle even more. What a good way to start the day.

Since Papa didn't talk very much, when he did speak to me, I paid careful attention; it was probably important. Filling our water gourds one day, Papa put his hand on my shoulder and told me to be kind to Paris, to work hard, and to listen carefully to every word that Paris said to me. "But Moses, don't ever repeat anythin' that Paris says to you, except to your Mama and me; I mean don't *ever*! Do you hear me, son?"

"Papa, I promise." I would do just exactly what he had told me to do. My father was a good man and I wanted to make him proud of me. Papa was born on the Porter Plantation. When they were children, he and Massa played together as they were about the same age. That is where the likeness ended. My father was always a thoughtful man, with a talent for fixing broken things: farm equipment, faltering crops, a horse that had lost its shoe, a broken wheel on the wagon, and teary-eyed children. I don't know what Massa was like when he and Papa played together as children, but I do know what he was like on the plantation. Not quiet. Not thoughtful. Not kind. He was not at all like Papa.

Funny thing about what Papa said to me that morning: every day he told me to be kind to Paris and to work hard, but that last part about listening to Paris was new.

Paris always took my hand as we walked the long trek from our cabin to the barn on the far side of the Big House. We took these same steps every day, sometimes counting them just to pass the time. Paris only knew how to count to twenty and that's what he taught me, so we just kept counting to twenty over and over again, stepping in kind of a rhythm as we said the number aloud with each step. It probably was more than twenty times that we counted to twenty, but I never did stop to figure that out then.

I thought I was a little too big for holding hands, but if it made Paris happy, I was happy to oblige him.

Paris had been married once. People always said that his wife was as beautiful as a queen, and as kind as she was beautiful. She died in childbirth, along with their child. Mama regularly told me that Paris was lonely, and I am sure now that he was. He didn't talk to me about his wife, but every once in a while, her name, Peace, just crept into our conversations.

It was going to be a sun-shiny day, and though it was just barely dawn, the cardinals and chickadees were already chirping away, singing to each other as if they hadn't a care in the world. Paris cheerfully mimicked the loud, clear whistle of the red cardinal and the *fee bee fee bee* song of the chickadee. Every morning I tried to do it as well as he did, but I was not very good.

As we neared the creek, the tiny Virginia bluebells lit up our path with their soft blue and pink flowers, telling us that spring was finally here. The May sun had warmed the soil after the long, cold winter.

"Well, Moses. I guess we better pick up our feet and get movin'. Those horses, mules, and cows are goin' to want to get out of that stuffy barn and into this clear, crisp spring air."

"Yep, Paris. Let's get a move on."

Paris let the cows out into the alfalfa pasture while I opened the heavy and bulky barn doors, letting the horses and mules into the field. Paris called out to me, "Moses, did you put smashed corn out for the chickens yet?"

"No, Paris, on my way to do that now."

Once all of the animals were out of the barn, we were ready to clean up after them inside the barn. "Let's muck out these stinky stalls, put down some sweet-smellin' new hay, and get 'em fresh water, son." Together we made ten trips hauling dirty hay out behind the barn to a place in the sun where it would dry; only then could we chop it into bitty teensy pieces to spread onto our vegetables for fertilizer. The job seemed to take forever and I was getting mighty tired. Each time I heaved a pitchfork full of the heavy, smelly hay out into the yard, the handle slid up and down in my hands. Soon I had bloody, open blisters all over both hands. "Paris, I can't do this anymore. Look at my hands. They sting like crazy. Please, can't we take just a little break?" Paris shot me a look that said "no". And, it was a look that told me he meant it. I knew Paris was tired too, but he never admitted it. He just accepted that he really had no choice…keep going.

I took a couple of big gulps from my water gourd and encouraged Paris to do the same, while I scrambled over to our secret hiding place behind the corn crib.

There we had concealed a small covered pot that we called our 'For Later' pot into which we put a few fresh fruits or vegetables. There weren't many fresh fruits or vegetables ripe in May - we weren't permitted to share in the bounty of the Massa's gardens anyway- but there was asparagus that came up every year without anybody's help at all. Paris and I planted spring peas and strawberries back in February, so they were ready to pick.

We could only sneak one or two things from the gardens as we worked and then only things that were small enough to go into our pockets. Taking something from the gardens where we worked was considered stealing, since the land belonged to the Massa and not to us. If he had chosen to give us a few vegetables or fruits once in a while, we would not have been tempted to take anything.

On that day, we had strawberries, a few hard-boiled eggs, a

handful of peas, and some of Mama's good biscuits in our pot. The strawberries were already getting soft, so I brought them out to Paris, saving the eggs, biscuits, and peas for another time. Together we gobbled up those juicy, red berries as quickly as we could. Paris let out a big chuckle and remarked, "Moses, it'd be a good idea to wipe that juice off your face before Massa or Ben come by to pay us a visit!"

After putting down fresh hay in every stall, Paris told me, "Let's get Stubby and Piggy hooked up to the plows, Moses, so we can break up those fields."

Paris began plowing on one end of the field, and I started on the other end. We always did it that way so that when we were finished we would meet in the middle, share another swallow of water from our drinking gourds. We slapped each other on the back and kind of laughed as we made deep bows, pretending to be formal and fancy like Massa. Nobody else ever recognized a job well done, so we got used to congratulating each other.

I was working on my second row, making perfectly straight furrows, when I caught sight of something bright and sparkly lying on the ground just ahead of where the nose of the plow was digging into the dirt. It was catching the rays of the sun, glittering like that fancy diamond ring Missus Martha wore. Getting close, I leaned over just a little bit so I could pick it up. I thought I could get it without stopping Stubby who was plodding forward pulling the plow and me.

Leaning over.

Leaning over just a little more.

Leaning over even more.

Still more. Stubby paid no attention to me and just kept tramping along. "Oh, Paris, help!' I cried out as I fell, tipping the plow over with me as I hit the ground.

The ropes connecting the plow to the mule got tangled up with my hands and the nose of the plow as it flopped over. My left leg inched along in the dirt, under the frame of the plow while I used the heel on my other foot to dig into the dirt, trying to get that dumb mule to stop. Stubby just kept on goin', draggin' me with him.

"C'mon, Paris! Hurry!" I was hollering loudly by then. Finally, I was smart enough to let go of the plow, so I didn't get dragged any further, but Stubby was still absent-mindedly continuing on down the row.

We named the mules Stubby and Piggy because everyone said mules are stubborn and pig-headed. They are!

At long last, Paris got Stubby to stop. He came over to check to see if I was hurt. Bruises and muddy scrapes covered my left leg, from my knee to my ankle, and I wanted to complain. But, compared to the injuries Papa got in the tobacco fields, or the whippings Paris endured, I realized that my sore leg didn't amount to a hill of beans.

"Not hurt, Paris, but I am embarrassed. If I weren't so spindly or if I were a little stronger, Stubby wouldn't have had such an easy time with me."

31

"Well, boy, you sure made a mess of this field. What were you doin,' anyway?"

"I saw this shiny thing, Paris, and I wanted to pick it up. So, I leaned over just some, and that's how it all started." I explained.

"Well, did you get it?" Paris asked. "Was it worth it? Better show me that thing."

"Yeah, Paris. I got it! Grabbed it up out of this dirt as quick as a wink. It's definitely worth it. Look at it shining and sparkling in my hand. It's beautiful. Looks like a diamond to me. I think that sharp point on the end must be pointing at somethin.'"

"That sure is pretty, Moses. It's not a diamond, can't find those around here. But it is a good size piece of quartz, 'bout the size of a small egg. It's shiny because it has been tossed around in the dirt for a long, long time. Many, many years. I guess you were meant to have it. But now we gotta get back to work." We finished our day together putting oats in the bucket of each horse and mule stall, and putting corn in the cow stalls. We filled all the buckets with fresh water from the creek, and brought all of the animals into the barn for the night. We both made a quick, sneaky trip to the corn crib, and filled our pockets with cracked corn for our chickens before heading home. I always stuffed that corn deep down in my pockets so that none of it would fall out and give me away. I never forgot the day Massa discovered those carrots in Paris' pocket. That whipping was a bad one - something I never wanted to experience.

Walking slowly back to the slave quarters, Paris again took

my hand and asked me a question. "Moses, you heard about abolitionists?"

"I heard the big people whisper that word, but I don't know what it means."

"They are some white people in the North who know slavery is wrong. They talk about it in public places and some of those people try to help slaves run away to free states."

"What's a free state?"

"A place that doesn't allow slavery."

"Oh Paris, I didn't know that there was any place like that! I thought that every black kid was a slave like me."

I couldn't believe what I was hearing. I was beside myself. Paris was telling me things that I hadn't heard before - happy things. I felt like I could jump out of my own skin. *Why am I a slave, and some other kid is not?*

"No, Moses, every black child is not a slave. There are some places that have passed laws against slavery."

"Where are those free places?"

"In the North."

"How you know where 'North' is, Paris," I asked, confused. "Why don't I know this stuff, Paris? How come nobody told me?"

"I'm tellin' you now, Moses. You are old enough now to learn about these important things. You remember all those stories about the stars in the sky, and about that one special star that is called the North Star'? Well, if you walk and walk and walk followin' the North Star, you would be goin' north, Moses."

Rubbin' that stone back and forth in my hands, I was about to bust. My brain was racing with excitement. I could hardly stand still. *Imagine! Some black kids are free! Maybe I can get free. I'd have to go north to get free. How could I ever do that?*

"I am goin' to look for the North Star tonight, Paris."

"Oh, I just thought of another way to find out which direction is north, Moses."

"What's that?"

"Did you know that moss grows on the north sides of trees? That's because the sun doesn't shine there so much. One more way to find out where north is."

"I sure do want to be free."

"All of us do, Moses. But we must never talk about it. We just watch and listen. Maybe one day there will be a chance. I am too old to even think about runnin' away, and it doesn't seem worth it to me without Peace by my side any ol' ways. But I want you to think about it. You're young and smart, and you shouldn't be trapped on this plantation here all your whole life."

"I will, Paris. I will."

"Tonight we'll polish up that shiny quartz stone. I want you to keep it with you always. It will remind you every day that you want to be free. We'll call it your freedom stone. Now, no more talk about this, Moses."

"I know. I heard Papa tell me that this morning."

"I think your Papa knows I talk more than he does," Paris smiled. "He hopes that I will tell you important things that you must know, now that you are twelve years old," he added.

Passing by the apple orchard, Paris started to sing:

> *Swing low, sweet chariot,*
> *Comin' for to carry me home*

"Paris, I got a question for you," I looked into Paris' dark, friendly eyes.

"Shoot, go ahead; you always got a lot of questions, boy," replied Paris.

"How come we sing songs all the time when we are really not so happy?"

"Songs help us to get through the tough times. Songs help us to remember where we lived and who we were before we became slaves. And we got some secrets in those songs too. Careful now, son, I think I see Massa over there near the Big House. Keep walkin'. But no talkin' for a few minutes 'til we get past him," Paris warned.

When it was safe to talk again, Paris continued. "Those white folks don't know that when we sing 'carry me home,' 'home' really means 'freedom'. They just think it means 'heaven'; well, freedom would be heaven now, wouldn't it?"

"It sure would," I agreed.

We were almost back to the quarters when Paris said, "Now, I got a question for you, Moses."

I had to laugh. It was usually me asking all of the questions;

now Paris was turning that all around. "Go ahead, ask away," I answered.

"You know how important it is to Massa that everyone in the county knows about how rich he is, don't you? Did you ever think about just how he got so rich?"

"Well, no, I never thought about that."

As we talked, Paris' eyes darted from one side to the other, constantly checking to be sure that no one was anywhere near us. Both of us knew that our conversation was just for the ears on our two heads—no one else's. We rounded the last corner and stepped into our little section of the plantation, the slave quarters.

"Moses, the Massa makes a lot of money sellin' his tobacco because he does not pay slaves to do the work. If he had to pay people to do all the work that we do day and night around here, he would not be so rich and he wouldn't be able to brag to everybody about all of the stuff he owns, includin' that great big fancy house over there," Paris finished.

"Paris, you sure told me a lot of stuff to think about today. My head is spinnin' round and round, tryin' to understand it all."

"I know I have, but you are growin' up now and it's important to learn some of these things."

I must admit that, before my conversations with Paris, I hadn't given any thought to it. Slavery, that is. But, after that day, I thought about it all the time. I was obsessed with it. It just didn't seem right that one person could really own another person. Massa Porter owned me as sure as I sit here now writing our story. He owned me in the same way that he owned the animals in the barn. I was a slave. Massa didn't buy me like he bought my mother. I was his slave because I was born to slaves that he already owned.

"We've had a good day today, no visits from the Massa or Ben," Paris said, grabbing my hand more tightly. We headed toward the creek. "There's still a glimmer of light left. The moon is beginning to shine on the water. Let's see if we can get some fish for our dinner, Moses."

"OK, Paris. I'm not very good at fishin'. James and I have fished some, but I still haven't caught even one fish."

"About time you learned, son. I'm goin' to show you a good way to bring home somethin' good for dinner."

We got to the bank of Mill Creek, and Paris pointed to a spot where the creek narrowed. It was so narrow; we could almost jump across. Paris instructed me to find some large rocks so we could dam up the creek, making it even narrower than it already was. I searched for rocks along the edge of the creek and around the roots of some big trees. Grabbing one that I thought was

37

perfect, Paris laughed, "Moses, I'd call that a small stone. If you don't find anythin' bigger than that, it will take us all night to make the dam."

So, back I went to gather some larger rocks. I found one that was about twice the size of the first I had brought to Paris and he was pleased. "Good job, Moses. Get two more like that, and we will have enough." It took me some time, but eventually I delivered two more rocks to Paris, who placed them gently in the water so that there was only a small opening for fish to swim through.

"So, now we got a dam. What are we going to use to catch a fish, our hands? I asked.

Paris laughed. Well, actually sometimes you can get lucky that way. But, look," he said, pulling a small net from his back pocket."

I never knew you had that, Paris."

"Just keepin' you on your toes, son," he said.

"Now we'll put a small rock in the bottom of the net to weigh it down."

I handed him a stone and he showed me what to do next. Straddling two of the biggest rocks, he bent over and carefully wedged that net down into the opening. "Now, we wait," Paris said.

It seemed like it was taking forever and I was about ready to give up on the whole idea when Paris whipped that net straight up into the air. Inside was a pretty good-sized fish! I was ready to head back to the quarters for a tasty fish supper, but Paris suggested that it would be nice if we could catch one or two more fish to share. I wouldn't have dreamed of saying 'no' to him even if I wanted to. I remembered Papa telling me to listen to Paris and to do whatever he said. So, we stayed a little longer while I took a turn at placing the net into the crevice we had made. I wasn't as good at it as Paris, but he encouraged me and told me that I would get better at it with just a little more practice. I did not catch a fish that day, but Paris caught another and we happily headed for our home. We were hungry. The few berries from our "For Later" pot were all that we had eaten since breakfast.

After we finished our evening meal, I heard whistling from the pear tree grove near the slave quarters. It was James, my best friend. That whistle was our signal to each other whenever we wanted to get together. Telling Papa that I would be back in a little while, I dashed off to find James.

"Hey, Moses, I want to go fishing. Come along with me, I've got a great idea!" James suggested with a twinkle in his eye. I told him that I had just been fishing with Paris, but I never could turn down an opportunity to get into something with James. He always had tricks up his sleeve and it was fun to be with another kid, even though he was a little older than I. We climbed up on his horse, Thunder, and galloped off into the woods. When James was satisfied that we were far enough away that no one would see us, he grabbed the two fishing poles he had tied to the saddle, and we sat down on the shore of Mill Creek to wait for the fish to bite. James handed me two sugar cookies that Mama made earlier in the day. I never got to have treats like that so I gobbled them up quickly. It was a peaceful time, sitting there with my friend.

"James, whatever made you think that this was a good time to go fishin'?" I asked.

"Well, I'll tell you after we catch a big fish, not before," he replied. There was nothing for me to do but just wait. It wasn't too long before I caught a sizable fish. James was thrilled. I was too. It was the first fish I ever caught. "Now," he said, "here's the plan. Father is visiting Mr. Adams right now, and I think he will be gone for another hour or so." Using the heel of his boot, he stomped on that big ol' fish until he was sure that the fish was dead. "We're going to take this dead fish and hide it behind the largest books in Father's study. Pretty soon it will put out a smell that will make Father go berserk," he laughed.

I wasn't so sure that it was funny. "What will he do when he discovers it?" I worried.

"Oh, he won't discover it. After it has been stinking for a time, he will storm around the house hollering and complaining about it to all who can hear. I will be enjoying his rampage, I can assure you," James said.

"Mother is the one who will guess that I am the culprit," James continued. "Even though she will secretly think it is funny, she will feel that she must scold me and instruct me to get rid of the fish and its putrid smell. Regrettably, I will have to sneak into

40

Father's office, retrieve the dead fish and throw it into the creek."

James had a big smile on his face. "This is going to be so easy. I can't wait to hear him stomping and bellowing all over the place. I'll be laughing inside until my belly hurts," he laughed.

"Won't he know that you are the guilty one?" I asked.

"You know what, Moses? I really don't care if he does," James shot back.

I knew better than to say anything, but I couldn't help but worry. *James, you're going to be in trouble again. What will happen to you if Massa finds out? What if Massa thinks that I am the guilty one?*

CHAPTER FOUR

Quick Thinking Saves the Day
August 1851

Addie

"**A**deline, please come up to my room with me and Sarah." "Yes'm" I answered quietly. It was unusual for Missus to ask me to join her in her room. But I did as I was told even though I was a little bit frightened - more than a little bit actually - about what I might have done. Perhaps I had made a big mistake on the green silk dress that I had been working on for so long. Biting my lower lip as I slowly mounted the stairs, I worried.

Most times I worked alone upstairs on my sewing projects. Missus' spacious bedroom on the back of the Big House was fine, with the sunlight shining through the large windows overlooking the vegetable gardens where I could see Paris and Moses working. The fruit trees had finished flowering and were showing off magnificent ripe peaches and small apples that would soon be ready for harvest. Just beyond the fruit trees, the meandering Mill Creek babbled along over the stones and rocks.

Missus' dressing room was just off to one side with beautiful dresses hung on a rod placed near the ceiling. To get hold of one, I had to stand on a stool. Near the largest window stood an elaborate desk fit for a queen. It was at this desk that Missus taught Sarah reading, writing, and 'numbers'.

"I have something I would like to do with you today," beamed Missus. "Come along now over here to my desk, Adeline." Missus always called me by my formal name, Adeline. Everybody else called me Addie, except Mama, who used my full name when she was a little fussed at me. Massa didn't call me Addie or Adeline. He never once called me by my name. I only heard him call me "girl".

"Sarah and I would like to teach you to read and write, and we'd like to teach you your numbers too. You are a smart girl, and we think you should be able to do these things just as James and Sarah can. What would you think of that?"

"Oh, Missus," I whispered with absolute surprise and excitement. "I do want to learn. I have always wanted to learn. But it's against the law, isn't it?" I stammered, trying to catch my breath. I could hardly think. It seemed like a miracle; I might be able to learn to read and write!

"Yes, Adeline, it is against the law. Nobody is supposed to teach slaves to read or write. Each state has its own laws about it. In Virginia, it is against the law to try to educate slaves. So, we are going to have to be very careful to keep it a big secret. If anyone found out that you were learning to read and write, the punishment that the law allows is 20 lashes with the whip. And if it were discovered that I helped you to learn, I would be fined $100."

"Oh Missus, I don't want you to get in any trouble. That's a lot of money. I can't even imagine where anyone would put their hands on that much money."

"Adeline, let me worry about that. Now, please sit in that chair by the desk facing the door. Hold the dress and your needle and thread just so in your lap. If we hear Master William, or anyone, but especially him, coming up the stairs, you will quickly pick up your sewing, and quietly scoot your chair back toward the rod where my clothes hang, facing the opposite direction of Sarah and me. Meanwhile, we will continue with our lessons. Is this a good plan? Can you keep our secret?"

The surprise Missus sprang on me that day took my breath away. I was barely able to croak out my answer.

"Yes, Missus. I sure can keep a secret. You know that I can. You make me so happy."

My words came out sort of like rasping, and I almost cried. I held myself in check, but inside I was bursting with joy.

"Now, Adeline, there is another part of the secret. James and Moses have found a hiding place in the hayloft of the barn. James is teaching Moses to read and write in their concealed corner whenever they can find a few minutes here and there, without Ben Harrison or William finding out. They have been studying together for about two months now."

"Goodness, Missus," I gasped. "You would do this for us?"

"Yes, Adeline, it is the right thing to do," explained Missus. "But, mark my words, you and Moses should not even talk about it with each other. You must not even discuss it with your Mama, although she will probably figure it out for herself over time. Someone might just be within earshot and hear you. Do you understand? It is a very big, very important secret. Can you keep our secret?"

"Yes, Missus, oh yes missus, I promise I won't say a word!" I answered sincerely. It seemed like we were always being warned about not saying a word about anything to anybody. I never questioned that then and didn't really understand it. I simply listened. I always followed the rules.

Missus was a kind, good lady. From time to time when Massa was away, Missus would go out into the slave quarters, sit down on the ground with some of the children, or with Lavinia, an older slave who could no longer work in the fields. There she and Lavinia would chat like good friends while the children played jump rope, hide and seek, and rolled metal hoops in giant circles around the slave yard.

Missus always encouraged James, Sarah, Moses, and me to play together. We joined other children from the slave quarters in running competitions, sometimes girls against the boys, other times making relay teams. We all loved a game called Hide the Switch. We'd find a long, skinny limb as the switch, and one of us would take great pains to hide it so that the others would have trouble finding it. Whoever found the switch first chased after the rest of us, trying to 'switch' us. We didn't really 'switch' each other; we just had to touch the other person with the switch. The one who got switched first was the next to hide the switch again.

My first lesson was so confusing that I doubted if I was smart enough to ever learn anything. Missus opened a book called the English Battledore. On the first pages were things that she called "letters big and small," and other things called "consonants" and "vowels." There were columns of words that sounded alike; she called them "rhyming words" like "cat" and "rat" or "boy" and

47

"toy." Gently taking my pointer finger, she touched each letter or word and said it out loud to me, asking me to repeat after her. I did so, but truthfully, I had no idea what I was doing.

With Sarah's constant praise and encouragement ("That's good, Addie. You're doing fine, Addie."), Missus and I kept at it for some time. "I think that's enough for your first lesson, Adeline," Missus declared. "You did very well. I am so proud of you. Now, before we finish for today, I want you to close your eyes and try to make a picture in your mind of everything you saw in the book. Later, when you have a quiet moment, even if that has to wait until you get ready for bed, try to say the letters and words in your head. But not out loud. Remember what I told you about the importance of keeping this completely secret."

Within a month, I began to have some confidence that I really could learn to read. I was reading short, easy sentences or poems.

Do as well as you can, and do no harm.
Mark the man that doeth well, and do so too.
Help such as want help, and be kind.
Admit to your sins past, then mend.

Some of the words sounded a bit old-fashioned to me and without Missus' explanations, I would not have understood them. But I was reading! And once I understood the words of the poem, I knew those words were speaking about my Missus.

A few weeks later, Missus gave me a small slate and a piece of charcoal, warning me to hide it under my bed - a good, safe place since Massa never, ever ventured up into our attic room. She wrote a word and instructed me to copy it. My first attempts at writing were sloppy, at best. Gradually I began to improve. It seemed so complicated and overwhelming.

Too much to remember.

And I hadn't even yet begun to learn my numbers.

After we had worked together for about three months, I was learning all three: reading, writing, and numbers. I was so proud and excited that I wanted to share it all with Mama, but I had been warned. I knew that I mustn't breathe a word of my lessons to anyone.

Every day after we finished our lessons, Sarah and I enjoyed some play time together. Sometimes we played "I Spy." One of us would say to the other, "I spy with my little eye something red." Then the questions came rapid-fire. "Is it the red ribbon on that pillow on Mama's bed?"

"No."

"Is it the red sash Missus is wearing?"

"No."

We could play that game for a long time.

Occasionally we played a card game called "Memory." We put all fifty-two cards upside down in rows on the desk. Then we tried to find matching pairs. If we chose correctly, we got another turn. If we missed, the other got a turn.

Often, Sarah read to me. I always loved to listen to her sweet voice read fairy tales to me, wishing that I too could read. But now I was actually learning to read myself. Every once in a while, she asked me to read to her. Even though I knew that I could not read as well as she, it was with a feeling of pride that I did it.

Sometimes, we just made up stories to tell each other. We preferred silly stories, but once in a while we made up scary stories. That wasn't such a good idea, because I usually ended up having nightmares.

Every day when our lessons and play time ended, I skipped down the steps to join Mama in the kitchen, all the while singing to myself. It truly was the happiest part of my day.

> *I got peace like a river in my soul.*
> *I got a river in my soul.*
> *I got joy like a fountain in my soul.*

One day when I was running down the steps after my lessons, taking two at a time, and humming and laughing aloud when I didn't mean to, I ran smack dab into Massa. "This is an unusual turn of events, girl. What makes you so happy? It strikes me that you must not be working hard enough if you have time to be so light-hearted."

I had never before experienced such a moment. Feeling my

heart pounding so hard that I thought it would jump right out of my chest, I knew that I needed to come up with some excuse for my happiness.

If I waited too long to speak, Massa would suspect that I was up to something, something that he would not like, or approve of.

Without a clue where it came from, I answered, "I am so happy today, Massa. Missus has asked me to make a fancy dress for Sarah. There is to be a party for the children at the church and I am so lucky to make the dress that Sarah will wear. I have always made her clothes, but I have never been asked to make something so special as this dress," I stammered.

Massa at least thought about it for a minute before he grabbed me by my calico apron and steered me back up the staircase, where he confronted Missus who came out of her room in time to have heard our conversation.

"What is this all about, Martha? I don't remember hearing about any special party that Sarah is to attend," Massa exploded.

Missus was a quick thinker.

"William, I haven't had time to tell you about it. We have just recently learned about it and you have been so busy in your study. I didn't want to bother you," she replied.

Massa let go of me and clomped back down the stairs and into his study.

"Sarah, fetch your brother quickly," Missus instructed.

Within minutes, James was on his way to notify several friends about a special party that would be held in late September.

With a quick wink, Missus told me that she was certain that my Mama needed me in the kitchen.

What would have happened if Missus had not overheard my story? I was spared this time. But, what about next time?

CHAPTER FIVE

Fear Strikes the Quarters
September 1851

Moses

I t was Saturday night and we were hungry.

Really hungry.

The kind of hungry where your stomach just aches. The kind of hungry that saps all the energy right out of you. The women folk sang songs in an effort to keep their minds off of their growling bellies.

We gathered in the common yard created by the positioning of our four cabins, waiting for Ben, our crabby overseer, to deliver our weekly rations.

Papa, Paris and I took turns making up stories to try to get each other to laugh. Paris' stories were always about Africa; usually African stories don't have happy endings because that's where the slaves came from. But Paris always put some kind of comical, magical twist to his stories. He consistently got a laugh from all of us when he wrapped up his stories with the white slave catchers being the ones loaded onto the slave ships by the black Africans, instead of the other way around.

Papa loved tongue twisters. He repeated one several times before the rest of us could say the words with him. Then we said them faster and faster until it sounded like gibberish. One of my favorites was this easy one:

> *A skunk sat on a trunk.*
> *The skunk thought the trunk stunk.*
> *What stunk? The skunk or the trunk?*

My stories weren't really stories. I wasn't as creative as Papa or Paris. I was nervous about trying to make something up that might come out sounding silly or stupid. Instead, I picked a few rhymes from the reading book that I studied with James. Tapping out a rhythm on my handmade leather drum, I repeated the words over and over again in a musical fashion until everyone joined in.

A dog will bite a thief at night...a dog will bite a thief at night...a dog will bite a thief at night...a dog will bite a thief at night...

Or another...

Time cuts down all both great and small...time cuts down all both great and small...time cuts down all both great and small... time cuts down all both great and small...

When Ben arrived, you would have thought he was a king bringing gifts. He proudly sat on his horse, Snap, directing two of our strongest slaves, George and Cuffy, to bring the rations wagon up to the edge of the quarters. Then, with a flourish, he jumped down from his horse and shooed George and Cuffy away, as if to say, "Go now, you worthless slaves, your work here is done."

Ben doled out one pound of bacon, one peck of corn meal, one quart of flour, four sweet potatoes, and one small jug of milk per adult person. Children received a half-ration. Each cabin got one small crock of molasses and one of lard. I was the one from our cabin chosen to go up to Ben and ask him for our cabin's rations. Why does he make us ask? Seems mean. Ben stood over me as if he thought that I would take more than our share. It took me a few trips from the wagon to our cabin. Carrying the heavy jug of molasses on the last trip, I stumbled and fell. Some of the molasses oozed out onto the ground. While I was still on the ground, Ben marched over to me, his whip held high over his head, and sneered, "Now, look what you've done, you clumsy slave! Too bad that your cabin will have to make do with a half crock of molasses." I thought he was going to whip me, but, instead, he turned his back on me and walked away.

We had to live on these rations for seven days. We usually ran out by Thursday or Friday, no matter how hard we tried to make the food last. When there was food, I had cold bacon, corn grit cakes that Lizzie made from the corn meal, half of a sweet potato, and a small cup of milk.

Thank goodness for our truck patch, a small vegetable garden tilled and cared for by Lavinia. She planted potatoes, both white and sweet, zucchini and acorn squash, and onions: vegetables that stayed fresh for a long time. We saved some vegetables in large clay crocks in our cabins. Most were stored in the root cellar on the side of the hill near the creek where the soil was a little bit sandier and rain runoff would not seep into the cellar. Papa, George, and Cuffy dug the hole about three feet deep and flared out the sides at the top so it wouldn't cave in on itself. After lining the bottom with straw and dried leaves, they covered the hole with a heavy wooden lid. Over the lid the spread a thick layer of dirt.

Now and then we were fortunate to catch some good fish from Mill Creek and Massa did allow us to raise a few chickens.

We made do; we just barely made do. Nobody complained; that would just result in a whippin'. We just acted all thankful-like, even if we really weren't.

After the rations were distributed, Ben was done with his work for the week. He didn't work on Saturday nights or on Sundays. So as long as we were careful, we could pretty much have a good get-together in our slave community—our family. Mama and Addie were allowed to join us after the evening meal in the Big House; they even stayed the night with us (Addie and I slept on the floor when Mama stayed with Papa), as long as they reported back to the Missus in time to prepare Sunday breakfast. Each Saturday night, Mama hung on to Papa as if she hadn't seen him in a year, but it had really been just one week. "Mabry, Mabry, my sweet Mabry. You look so weary," she whispered to him as they held each other. At the time, I thought all that hugging and kissing was sort of silly, but I was only twelve then, what did I know?

Our gatherings on Saturday nights sometimes turned into real shindigs. At times the slaves from the Adams Plantation and those from Franklin Farm a few miles further away joined us, bringing with them some surprises such as a cake or a pie - scrumptious foods we rarely had. Mr. Adams allowed his slaves more food rations than we had on the Porter Plantation. The slaves on Franklin Farm shared the same food as the Franklin family. Each slave holder ran things according to his own rules.

Lizzie and Lavinia were the best cooks in the quarters, so they set about preparing a sturdy meal of sweet potatoes, corn bread, some snap peas that Paris sneaked in, and some fish that Henry, Elijah, and Robert caught in Mill Creek. Mama helped, but she usually was grateful for a little rest from cooking. The women asked some of us older boys to fetch water from our common well in the center of our carefully swept yard. We collected the water in clay jugs that we sometimes called memory jugs.

One of the slaves from the Adams Plantation was a pretty good fiddler. Reddick and Henry, from our plantation, joined him. Together they made up what we called our 'band.'

They liked to play lively music that would get everybody in a happy mood, jumping, clapping, and dancing to the music. Now and again they would play slow, somber tunes that seemed quite sad. I watched Mama. Tears ran down her pretty face. I wondered why the music made her so troubled. *Mama, why are you so sad?* When they played spirituals that we all knew, everyone sang along, rocking and swaying.

Cuffy, who worked as a carpenter, made two pairs of stilts for the children. We took turns, pushing and jabbing with a flimsy stick in our hands, trying to knock the other person off their stilts. When one person fell over, another person tried, until we finally had a champion. Addie was always the winner, the athlete in the family.

Cuffy also made a ride that he called the 'roundabout'. On top of a big 'ol tree stump, he drove a wedge down a way into the center and on top of that he placed a seven-foot long plank wide enough to sit on. The plank had a hole in it right in the center that fit right over that wedge. Elijah and I sat on the ends of the plank and Lewis gave us a whopping push and we went whirling and spinning around until we got so dizzy we had to stop. Elijah couldn't help himself, he just had to go ahead and say it, "Hey, Moses, remember that time you threw up on the roundabout? We were going around and around so fast that it flew right back at you and hit you in the face!" I didn't need to reminded of that embarrassing moment.

Some of the boys liked to play marbles, but I didn't like it because our marbles weren't real; ours were homemade so they weren't perfectly round. They didn't roll very well, and I was a little resentful, because I knew how good real ones were from when I played with James.

It got real peaceful-like when we all ate our supper together by the light of the fire and the moon. We were too busy eating to talk very much. The food was good; we were all thankful for our first filling meal of the week. Looking back on those Saturday nights, I remember being calm and comfortable, even cheerful.

One night, the coziness and contentment ended abruptly after supper when the grownups started talking. They huddled closer and closer together so they could talk almost in a whisper; we children crowded in so we could hear too. Some of the parents shooed the children away, instructing them to 'Go play.'

Papa allowed me to listen, but he put his finger in front of his lips reminding me to say nothing. Then he told me to quickly get a few of the other bigger boys to run to the creek with me carrying some of our bed blankets. We knew what we were supposed to do.

This wasn't the first time.

We dipped the blankets into the water and dragged them back as fast as we could. They were so heavy and we were just boys. We made a circle around the adults, holding our wet blankets as high in the air as we could to muffle the sounds of the adults talking. As they talked, my arms got weary holding a heavy, wet blanket high above my head for so long.

I became terrified as the tale unraveled.

George, the blacksmith, had a written pass to go into town to get supplies for the fences and gates he was making for the Massa. While there, he overheard some white people in the shop talking about a slave running away from the Adams' plantation. As soon as Master Adams' overseer discovered the slave missing, he hurried to tell the Master. The Master instructed the overseer to ride as fast as possible to hire the slave catchers, rough, wild-looking men who had dogs that could track a person's scent. The two slave catchers came around to the Adams' slave cabins to let the dogs catch a scent of the boy's straw mattress; then off they went to try to find the boy. They headed straight into the woods where they thought he would have run. But they couldn't get a scent and they found no evidence of the slave anywhere. After a few hours of dashing all around and finding nothing, they sat down on a hefty log to rest. And, that's when it happened.

Because it was so quiet, the runaway thought he was safe to come out of his hiding place in the creek. The water sloshing over his pant legs made just enough noise to startle the dogs. They started barking and howling as they raced after the boy. Following as closely as they could, the slave catchers finally caught up with the dogs and the runaway as one of the dogs had the boy's shirt in his jaws. After the boy was returned to Frederick Adams, he was soundly whipped by the overseer, over and over again, the leather strap tearing through his clothes making huge, bloody gashes on his back, legs, and ankles. The whipping continued until the boy could no longer stand. As he fell to the ground, his mother ran to him, wailing, but she was back-hand-slapped so hard by the overseer that she too tumbled, and lay next to her passed-out son in front of their cabin.

This story made my heart race. My mouth was so dry, I had to keep running my tongue around. I knew that Massa and Ben would now be even harder on us. They thought that being mean and strict would encourage us to work harder and would discourage us from running way. Funny thing they didn't know; it just didn't work that way. We might have been interested in working harder and less interested in running away if the two of them were as kind and nice as Missus.

The disturbing conversation lasted until the children were tired and everyone slipped quietly into their own cabins for the night. But Mama, Papa, Paris, Lizzie and Lafayette made sure that Addie and I understood that what was said that night must be kept to ourselves. Papa told me again for about the millionth time, "Moses, don't ever repeat what you hear in the quarters. Understand? If you talk about these things, you could end up gettin' someone in trouble by mistake."

Papa always said, "Eyes and ears open, mouth closed." "I know, Papa." I reassured him that I would not breathe a word of it to anyone. But that awful scene stuck in my brain like glue. I just had to think about it some. *What am I going to do, knowing such gruesome things happen when people try to escape slavery?*

Sunday mornings meant that we had to get nice and cleaned up because we had a little praise time in our yard right after our breakfast. Lafayette seemed to know a lot about the Bible so he always talked gently to us about how Moses led his people out of slavery in Egypt, about the story of Jesus, and about the message "You will be saved." That particular Sunday, I think we really needed to hear Lafayette's calming words.

After Lafayette finished his message, we all sang together swaying to the rhythm of the music.

I got wings, you got wings,
All o' God's chillun got wings.
When I get to heab'n I'm goin' to put on my wings,
I'm going to fly all ovah God's Heab'n.

Chapter Six

The Christmas Party
December 1851

Addie

The tobacco had been sold at the market and it was not yet time to begin planting for the next year's crop. For field slaves, winter work was less strenuous than during the growing season, but they were certainly not sitting around doing nothing. The usual rule of working sunup to sundown was altered on our plantation just for this one month; field slaves started working around nine in the morning and ended their workday about four in the afternoon.

Because tobacco was so hard on the land, new fields had to be prepared every winter by clearing trees and burning the underbrush.

Massa had recently learned about a new method for drying tobacco. This involved building a shed called a 'curing barn' where the tobacco leaves would be hung in bunches from the ceiling and dried by the warmth of hot coals. This was going to work very much like the smokehouse back behind the barn where the meat for the plantation was hung from the ceiling.

This year, after cutting trees from an area quite far from the quarters, some of the field slaves had to split the logs, carry them to the site where the new curing barns would be built, and then begin to build the sheds.

Others spent their workdays mending fences around the plantation property.

Some helped Paris and Moses spread fertilizer in the vegetable gardens and over the old, soon to be unused, tobacco fields. Moses explained to me that if the fields were fertilized, it was possible to re-use the field after 8-10 years; if it was not, the field had to remain fallow for 20 years. I guess that's why Massa owned so much land; so much of it could not be used.

But Mama and I did not have it easy this time of year. Massa and Missus would be entertaining family and friends during the holidays, so we spent our days cooking and baking.

Cooking and baking.

Cooking and baking.

It was never-ending. Polish the silver. Wipe the crystal glasses with spotlessly clean soft cloths to make them shine. Clean the house from corner to corner...not our usual weekly cleaning, but going into every little nook and cranny searching out any tiny speck of dust. Massa, not Missus, was the inspector. We'd better not miss anything!

Any spare minutes that I was able to save for myself, I spent making new clothes for Sarah and Missus.

Though I was tired, I did enjoy the sewing times. I was alone with my own thoughts while I worked. And I was making beautiful dresses. While I worked, I could daydream about a time when I might be able to wear dazzling dresses. It was so quiet up in Missus' grand room. Peaceful.

The first party of the holiday season was planned for the second Saturday of the month. Early one morning, Missus asked Mama and me to help her with the decorations. She sat with us in the warm kitchen. While she and Mama enjoyed a cup of coffee together, she told us how she would like to decorate the house.

We were ready for a nice break from our routine. James hitched Thunder up to a spacious wagon. He toted us all over the plantation as we filled the wagon to the top with small branches of holly, loblolly and Virginia pine, cedar and spruce. "James, over there! Take us there to those big magnolia trees. Missus will like those big, fat, shiny green leaves," Moses called out. "Okay,

okay, Moses, here we go." And he took off at a tear. With Moses and James whooping it up, Mama and I hung on to the sides of the wagon for dear life. Finally, James brought the wagon to a halt. "Moses and I will cut magnolia limbs. Addie, you and your Mama fill this muslin bag with as many pine cones as you can," James instructed. It was fun running all around the grounds of the plantation, searching for pine cones. "Mama, I'm going to find the biggest one," I challenged. "Oh no, you're not, I am," Mama replied.

We got mighty messy and sticky from the tree sap, but it was such an adventure. As we bounced along, we sang songs as loud as we could, hoping our voices would cheer any slaves who might be within earshot.

With James astride Thunder, and Mama, Moses, and I crammed in the wagon with all of the fragrant Christmas greens, we were a sight.

James directed his horse to the edge of Mill Creek so we could stir up all of those greens in the water to remove any dirt or bugs. We did the same with the pine cones. Shaking the water off after the greens and pine cones were clean, we spread everything out on a large canvas 'paulin to dry in the warm, bright sunlight. Mama had the biggest pine cone, course we hadn't decided on any special prize, so it was just braggin' rights. We returned and piled the clean evergreens and pine cones back into the wagon for the short ride back to the house.

Greens were everywhere in the house. Mama and Missus

made four wreaths, each wreath featured a variety of greens, pine cones, and apples...one for the front door, another for the back door, and two for the fence posts out at the road. Arrangements of greens decorated the dining room table, the big buffet, and all of the side tables in the parlor. The staircase was trimmed with draping garlands of greenery, onto which we tied beautiful glass ornaments that Missus ordered from England.

I never saw so many candles. Missus must have had close to fifty candlesticks of all sizes. We placed candles of varying heights on every table, shelf, and mantle.

James, Moses, and Cuffy cut down an enormous tree which they placed in front of the big windows in the parlor. This was only the second year that the Porter Plantation enjoyed a Christmas tree and I thought it was so exciting to watch it being hauled into the house and put up on a floor stand made of two boards nailed together in the form of an X. And it smelled so good! Mama and I made cookies of all shapes, mostly stars, to hang on the tree. We made paper roses for the tree. Other tree decorations included nuts, candies, apples, colorful glass balls, and of course, candles.

I closed my eyes and said to myself, "One day I will have my very own Christmas tree!"

A few slaves were carefully selected to care for the guests at the party including Moses, Papa, Lafayette and George. Counting Mama and me, we were six servants. Mama and I would serve the food. Papa and George were to greet the guests when their carriages arrived, help the ladies step down from the carriages, and escort them into the house. Lafayette would take coats and hats and place them in the closet.

Reddick and Henry were chosen for their fiddling talent, Reddick on the banjo and Henry on the fiddle.

We were all decked out in the frilliest and fanciest clothes that had ever been on our backs. I had no idea where Missus got these clothes; I didn't make them. I thought we looked pretty foolish, but it seemed to make Massa proud that we cleaned up so good.

The guests arrived to a house lit everywhere with candle-light. The fragrance of the greenery and the aroma of the food being prepared in the kitchen made the house smell wonderful. Reddick and Henry welcomed the guests to the house with bright and cheery music. Everything seemed to be perfect.

And it was.

Mama and I carried the roasted turkey, cold boiled ham, beets, winter squash, fried celery, turnips, and potatoes to the table. The twenty-four guests seemed to marvel at the buffet we had prepared. I confess that I felt more than a little bit proud of the grand spread of food on the table decorated so beautifully, and lit with seven tall candles amid the greens.

The guests complimented Missus about the food and how beautiful the house looked. Massa shot Missus one of those looks when she gushed, "Oh, thank you so much, but I cannot take the credit. That is due Rebecca and Adeline." Fortunately for Missus and for us, there were too many people around for him to say anything nasty just then. Mama and I smiled a tiny little smile and nodded our heads, lowering our eyes so that we wouldn't look directly into the faces of the guests. We knew that we weren't supposed to do that.

After dinner, Reddick and Henry entertained Massa's and Missus' friends charmingly when they requested certain songs and dances. The rum punch bowl was filled and re-filled many times.

Everything was splendid.

"Everyone, gather around here in the dining room. Tonight, we have a very special dessert," Missus said to her guests.

As everyone circled the extravagant table, Mama and I carried out the mince pies, each lit with a circle of small candles. Proudly carrying the pies and enjoying the oohs and aahs of the guests, I failed to watch where I was going. I tripped on a corner of the rug and fell to the floor, trying my best to hold the pie upright. As I struggled to get up without dumping the pie all over the floor, I did not notice that the candles on the pie had caught my apron afire.

The guests gasped.

Missus ran to my side, helped me back into the kitchen where she ripped my apron from me and plunged it into the big pot of water we kept at the stone hearth.

Somehow Mama managed to keep calm. After placing her pie on the table, she came back into the kitchen and rushed to see if I was ok. When she was certain that I would be fine, she made three more trips out to the table with more candlelit pies.

Thankfully, Reddick and Henry took note of what was happening, and started up with their happy holiday music again to keep the company in good spirits. Guests refilled their punch glasses and moved back into the parlor for more singing and dancing.

Massa barged into the kitchen. I had never seen him in there before. With clenched teeth trying to keep his voice low so that his guests would not hear him, he hissed at me. "You have embarrassed me in front of my friends! They must think that I don't know how to train my workers. Martha, I expect you to deal with this ignorant child! But, you...you...you...." He shot me one of those looks of his, while he was trying to figure out what he wanted to say next. I guess he couldn't come up with anything because he just seethed, "For tonight, do not come out of this room until everyone has gone home."

He turned and stomped out. I was ashamed. I felt as if I had disappointed Missus. I wanted to cry, but I did as I always did, lowered my head. Missus wrapped her arms around me and whispered, "Enough of this now, Adeline. It was an accident. I consider it over and done with." She smiled at me as she left the kitchen to join her guests. Such was Missus' way of "dealing" with me.

If it had been Massa, I would have been so scared. Would he have hit me like I saw him hit Missus?

Christmas in the quarters was quite different from the celebrations in the Big House. No fancy decorations. No glass balls decorating a tree.

Still we managed to find moments of joy during the holiday season. Massa allowed eight days' rest from our work, from Christmas Eve to New Year's Day. The amount of time off that slaves enjoyed differed from one plantation to the next.

On the Adams Plantation, slaves found a large, slow-burning log from the woods to burn in the parlor fireplace of their big house, which they called the 'manor house.' The number of days off depended on how long the Yule log burned. The slaves chose the Yule log very carefully, hoping to find one that would burn for many days because as soon as the fire went out, they were back to work. We knew that the slaves on the Franklin Farm were allowed only three days.

In order to keep us under Massa's control, Ben constantly reminded us that Massa might change his mind at any time and completely take away the few days we were allowed to celebrate the Christmas holiday.

Some used the vacation days holding quilting bees (both men and women), making small quilted items such as dolls, tiny round table mats where one might place a candlestick, bags, large tablecloths, and crazy quilt bed blankets. Missus saved all of the scraps from the clothing, draperies, and bed coverings I made and gave them to everyone in the quarters. Others produced handicrafts from wood, whittling small figures, wall pictures, or bowls.

Mama and I did not have to work in the Big House on Christmas Day, so we enjoyed spending the day in the quarters with Papa and Moses and all of our friends. Massa, Missus, James, and Sarah, dressed in their finest clothing, visited us in the quarters, bringing gifts. I have no idea why they thought it necessary to dress up so special to come to the quarters. Surely, we didn't have any fancy Christmas clothes. Maybe they felt good about themselves, seeing the enormous contrast between how they looked and how we looked.

I studied my good friend Sarah. She looked beautiful in her floor-length skirt and the tightly fitted waist jacket buttoned all the way up to her long, slender neck. Her colorful bonnet matched the color of her skirt. Then I looked up and down at myself. I was wearing a gray, long-sleeved plain house dress covered by a white apron. Where Sarah's bodice had beautiful buttons, I had none. Of course, I had sewn everything Sarah wore, so I was proud of the look she presented when she entered the quarters. Yet I wished I had something so beautiful to wear on this special holiday.

We were not allowed to give gifts to Massa and his family. I didn't understand that, but Mama explained, "If we gave them gifts as they give us gifts, that would make us equals. That would never do, my child."

74

We were grateful for whatever we received. The men and boys received britches and hats, and the women and girls were given dresses and bandanas.

The best gifts were the food items that were not included in our normal diet. Beef, turkey, ham, apples, oranges, Hoppin' John (black-eyed peas and rice) or ashcakes (boiled cornmeal sweetened with molasses and wrapped in cabbage leaves to bake). Each year our food presents were slightly different from the year before, depending on what the Massa and Missus found to be readily available.

Massa, Missus, James, and Sarah stayed long enough to have dinner with us. Massa delivered homemade liquor to the men folk and wished us a Merry Christmas as they departed the quarters for the more comfortable and elegant holiday decorations of their own home. We celebrated into the wee hours.

Slaves were not allowed to drink at any other time of the year. Being unaccustomed to alcohol, many of our slaves drank too much, giving Massa the opportunity to tell us that without his rules, all slaves would be good-for-nothing lazy drunks.

Like slaves in other plantations, Henry took advantage of the Christmas holiday to visit his wife who had been sold to the Franklin Farm. Massa, and most slave owners gave their slaves written passes to leave the grounds to pay holiday visits to family members. Mama told me that when Henry's wife was sold away, there was a lot of wailing and weeping amongst all of the Porter slaves.

Reddick's wife and children had been sent all the way to South Carolina. It was too far away for a holiday visit. While everyone was singing and dancing, we didn't notice that Reddick was missing. I had heard stories about slaves escaping at Christmas time. If they were stopped along the road, they simply had to show their passes as an explanation of why they were away from their slaveholder. Running away on Christmas Day gave runaways a days' head start before they would be discovered missing.

Papa was the first to discover that Reddick was gone. That was the end of the celebration. Papa calmly gathered us in a prayer circle, where we prayed that Reddick would find his way to his family. We prayed that he would not be caught and returned to the Porter Plantation where Ben would surely deliver the worst punishment we had ever seen.

I had trouble falling asleep. I could only think of Reddick and his family. *Oh, Reddick, please be careful. I hope you make it to South Carolina. I hope you find your family. I am so afraid. What if Papa decides to run away with Mama, Moses, and me? What would happen to us?*

CHAPTER SEVEN

Ben's Revenge Hits Home
July 1852

Moses

The days were long and tiring in the hot sun. Papa and the others worked their own rows, watching out for Ben who rode around the fields, sometimes even riding on his horse up and down each row, just so he could yell at everyone. He always had his whip at his side, just in case someone might look at him funny or if someone was working too slowly.

He really flashed that whip around, snapping it as a warning, should anyone do something to displease him.

Now and again, Ben chose one slave to give big trouble to, whipping him senseless just to show the others that he meant business. Papa told me that one rainy day Ben watched as Exeter, a field slave like Papa, stopped occasionally to wipe the rain from his eyes with the handkerchief from his pocket. Ben shouted as he cracked the leather whip, "One more time you stop and take another break, you will feel the sting of this!"

Though Papa was so skinny—thin as a rake—, he worked just as hard and fast as some of the men who were much sturdier types. I was tall and slender too, but not as muscular as Papa. Perhaps because he had such a thin body, the muscles on his arms stood out. I was envious of his obvious strength, and I often tried to flex my muscles to see if I could make them bulge out of my arm like his.

He usually sang and hummed to himself as he worked, thinking about better times to come.

I was worried about Papa.

For several days, he hadn't seemed like himself. He was not singing anymore. He was not giving me his usual morning speech about listening to Paris and about keeping my mouth shut when it came to stuff I heard in the quarters. He was a little slow-moving and he didn't want to eat anything.

Lafayette told me that Papa vomited several times out in the field when they were working. He was getting weaker and weaker every day. Paris warned me that maybe Papa was not going to get better.

I didn't want to hear that.

I pretended there was nothing wrong with him.

Papa was a brave man and he got up early every morning and worked in those fields, even though he was not feeling well. Lafayette told me that Ben started to be pretty hard on Papa those days when it was obvious that he was working slower and slower. The other field slaves tried to help Papa with his work, so he wouldn't get into any trouble.

One day he had a particularly bad day in the fields, hand-picking the horn worms off of the tobacco plants, one by one, a job that had to be done every day in July so the crop would not be ruined. He used to explain it to me, "Pick 'em off, then squash 'em with your shoe." Sometimes those worms were about the size of Papa's index finger. I thought it sounded like a sickening job.

Cruel ol' Ben was sitting at the end of Papa's row, astride his horse Snap, just waiting for an opportunity to give it to Papa.

Sure enough.

It happened.

Papa's legs weren't working just right and he was a little dizzy from the hot sun, from not having eaten, and from vomiting many times. He stumbled and fell to the ground right over one of Massa's precious tobacco plants, crushing it badly.

Ben slapped Snap's hind end; they flew down the row,

heading right for Papa.

"Get up, you lazy nigger!" barked Ben. "Look what you have done! Massa is not going to be happy about this!"

He pulled out that horrible leather strap that he used for whippings and he began flogging Papa around his legs and back.

When Lafayette was telling me all of this, I couldn't help myself. I tried to blink back my tears, but, once the first one rolled down my cheeks, it opened the flood gates.

He told me that Papa tried to keep from screaming, but finally he let out one long and deep howl. Tears streamed down his face. As his blood was running into the furrow, Ben stopped and yelled, "Take him to his bed. Then get back to work!" Israel and Exeter gently lifted Papa and carried him back to his cabin in the quarters.

Ben put the leather strap back on his waist and rode off down the row all the while bellowing at the slaves who had stopped working to watch what was going on. "What are you gawking at? You're supposed to be working, you lazy good-for-nothings!"

I don't think Ben had a heart, but if he did, it was as cold as stone.

Israel came running for me and together we ran to the Big House for Mama and Addie. Massa heard us crying and calling out to Mama and Addie. He asked Israel to tell him exactly what had happened. After Israel related the tragedy to the Massa, Massa got all red in the face and we could tell that he was angry. I couldn't tell if he was angry at us, or at Papa, or at Ben.

Paris, Lafayette, Lizzie, Mama, Addie, and I sat by Papa's bedside all night, listening to him struggling to catch a good breath. Early in the morning, Paris sent me to the big house to ask Massa to get the doctor. I ran as fast as I could, crying all the way. Massa had sent for the doctor a few other times when a slave was ill, and I hoped he would do it again now. James told me that some doctors wouldn't treat slaves. Others wouldn't treat slaves in the quarters, requiring that the sick slave be moved to the yard of the big house for treatment.

I was so afraid about Papa.

I banged on the door of the Big House so hard that my hand hurt. Massa opened the door. The words spilled out of my mouth so garbled that I am not sure the Massa even understood them. Tears were streaming down my face; I kept trying to wipe them with my shirt-sleeve.

Massa did send for the doctor who came later that day, but by then it was too late. Papa was gone.

Mama and Addie sobbed and wailed so loud that it made my head hurt. Mama just kept on hugging and hanging on to Papa, as if he could sit right up and talk to her.

She kept crying out his name, "Mabry! Mabry!" as she lovingly wiped his face with the gentle touch of the soft pads on her fingers.

Most all the other women folk were crying and moaning too, as they rocked back and forth in a slow, sad rhythm. The men folk were very quiet. Some just sat there with glum faces resting on their field-weary hands, so nobody could see their eyes. Maybe they were crying too and they didn't want us to know.

We felt each other's pain. We were in this together. Slavery had created our community. In a way, we were all in the same family.

Israel and Cuffy just seemed angry; they kept shaking their heads and slapping the table, or punching at the walls of our cabin. Reddick, Exeter, and Flemming quietly hummed and sang some of the songs that Papa always used to sing as he worked in the fields. And Lafayette tried his best to comfort all of us by telling stories from the Bible. His voice was steady as a rock and as deep as the river. I think Lafayette was trying to take over for Papa as the one person who could calm everybody else down in times of trouble.

When Cuffy got his angry self under control, he drifted over to Mama and in a whisper told her that he would start right away to make a box to bury Papa in. Mama nodded her head up and down, and for some reason, patted Cuffy on his head.

George, Henry, and Exeter approached Mama next to let her know that they would get all the field slaves started on digging Papa's grave. Lizzie gave Mama a big hug as she told her that she and Lavinia would help Mama to prepare Papa's body for burial.

I felt a heaviness in my chest that seemed like Stubby decided to sit right down on top of me. Or maybe it felt like I ate a dried up tough ol' piece of meat and I couldn't swallow it down. Or maybe it just felt like I might throw up.

I loved Papa so much.

His quiet ways had always made me believe there would be a better day, not maybe that day, but someday. Papa's few, but well-thought-out words normally helped me to understand that place where we lived and to learn about my peoples' past before we all became slaves, and to concentrate on a future time when I might be free.

I wanted to cry like Mama and Addie; maybe I would have felt a little bit better if I could have. I thought I shouldn't cry. I thought I should try to act like a man. Maybe I was cried out. I was also angry like Israel and Cuffy. I wasn't angry at Papa; I was just hopping mad at Ben, Massa Porter, and this thing called slavery. What happened to Papa was all wrong.

I didn't know what to do or what to think.

I shifted over closer to Paris who was sitting on the run-down old chair next to the table where he was carving something from a piece of wood. As I approached him, Paris stopped what he was doing and reached out for my hand. On all those early mornings when Paris held my hand as we were walking to the barn for our daily work, I thought I was a little too big to be holding hands, but on the day that Papa died, I was thankful to have his warm hand holding mine. Just sitting there with Paris lifted my spirits a little bit. Paris had been through all of this grieving business when his wife and baby died. He was a comfort to me then, and I can still feel his warmth as I tell you about that awful day.

Cuffy made a first-rate pine box worthy of Papa and he set it up on trestles made by George and Israel out of unused boards found behind the barn. Papa was gently laid inside the box; the lid was noiselessly closed. Addie and I stepped out into the common ground in the quarters, grabbing the hands of the other slave children who were old enough to join in. All together there were nine of us: Lewis, Peter, Elijah, Emma, Delia, Robert, Mingo, and of course Addie and me. Slowly, but purposefully, we began walking around Papa's box singing,

Free at last, free at last,
Thank God I'm free at last.
Free at last, free at last,
Thank God I'm free at last.

Over and over we sang the words as we encircled Papa's box. It seemed like we sang forever, but as the day turned into the pitch darkness of night, slaves from nearby plantations and farms arrived, some carrying lit torches. I tried to count how many people joined in, but I lost track after about seventy-five. It made me feel warm and glad inside that Papa was admired and respected by so many.

Cuffy, Henry, George, Robert, Hanson, and Flemming

carried Papa's box, leading the whole bunch of us in a procession escorting Papa to the lonesome slave graveyard, beyond the tobacco fields. It was a long walk for this crowd of sad slaves, one that we had walked several times before. Grief made our steps slow and heavy; gloomy thoughts and upsetting memories filled our heads as we made our way by the light of the torches to the place where we would bury Papa.

After Papa was gently laid in the grave, Lafayette spoke a few reassuring words about how we would all be free one day.

We circled the grave, shouting, chanting, and singing.

One by one, we each threw a clump of dirt onto Papa's box.

The men used shovels to finish burying Papa's box.

Mama silently placed Papa's cap next to the grave. Addie offered a beautiful seashell that had been a gift from Sarah. Paris added his woodcarving, bearing Papa's name and the date of his death. I placed Papa's drinking gourd on the soft earth. Papa was born on the Porter Plantation in Culpeper, Virginia. Now, he was buried there.

Locking arms, we headed back to our cabins, by the light of the torches and the moon, singing all the way.

> *Do Lord, o do Lord,*
> *O do remember me.*
> *Do Lord, o do Lord,*
> *O do remember me.*

The women put out a spread of food. Enjoying the good meal and the company of our good friends, gradually our grief gave way to celebration, as we shared our memories of Papa. It was so hard to believe he was gone.

All of a sudden Cuffy started laughing so hard that the rest of us just couldn't help ourselves and we started laughing too even though we had no idea what Cuffy was breaking up over.

"I'll never forget that time Mabry played that trick on Ben!" Cuffy shrieked. Though Papa was real serious-like, always talking in a hushed whisper, he did like to have a big hearty laugh once in a while. I had never heard about any times where Papa played tricks on anyone, let alone Ben, and I couldn't wait to hear the story.

Mama, George, and Lavinia were already doubled over in hilarity, but the rest of us still had no idea what was so funny. When he was able to catch his breath, Cuffy launched the tale.

"Sometimes Mabry was as sly as a fox," Cuffy began. "Ben was kinda sweet on a gal from the Adams plantation. She was a white indentured servant - worked in the big house with the Mistress. Ben was eager to get her in his cabin, talked about it all the time," Cuffy cracked up, holding his sides.

"Mabry had an idea." Cuffy continued. "Told Ben that he would ask your Mama to make a nice dinner basket so he could take that gal for a romantic picnic. He added that since Becca knew so much about herb medicines and hoodoo, he'd ask her to put in some of that love potion stuff that everybody called jalap root.

"'Now, listen here, Ben,' Mabry warned, 'got to take that love potion before your lady gets here so it has time to do its work.'

"And, by and by, your Papa got another idea.

"He offered, 'Ben, take that little fishin' boat us slaves use and take her on a little trip down the creek, until you come to that clearin' near the round top mountain. Be a nice spot for a romantic picnic. Sure to win her heart.'

"Thanking Mabry for the good suggestions, Ben went back to his cabin to spruce himself up. After telling your Mama of his plan, Mabry slipped on down to the creek and loosened one of those old boards on the bottom of the boat, didn't take it out, mind you, just gave it a little bit of loosening.

"None of us went with Ben and his lady friend, but Mabry and I went out ahead and hid high up in a tree over the round top.

"We could hardly stand it, we wanted so bad to bust out laughing; but of course, we couldn't. We knew that the love potion Mabry described to Ben was going to give him the runs. We just didn't know how long it would take.

"We watched Ben and his lady friend get all settled on a blanket. They spread out their picnic. Then, without any warning, Ben jumped up, grabbed all the picnic stuff and that gal and they hopped back in the boat as fast as a jackrabbit - quick as lightning.

"Pulling those oars as fast as he could, he didn't notice that the boat was filing up with water until they were both wet up over their ankles. The boat didn't quite make it back to Ben's house before she hopped out of there and ran off. Ben just sat there, messing his pants and cussing about the sinking boat."

I still can't believe that my Papa was the instigator of such an outlandish trick. However, I always knew how all of us in the quarters felt about Ben, that mean, poor excuse for a man. The merriment was just what we needed to break our sadness.

Everyone seemed to enjoy hearing that story and it did lighten the mood in the quarters. But by the time Cuffy was near the end of the tale about Ben, I began thinking about something terrible.

Ben was probably furious at Papa after the boat incident. He vowed to get revenge. He waited for just the right time. When Papa got sick and fell on the tobacco plant, Ben took advantage of the opportunity to get back at Papa. That's when he whipped him over and over again. I don't know if Papa would have lived if he had not been beaten, but I think the whippings made him worse. He killed Papa's spirit. Yes, I think Ben was responsible for Papa's death.

Once I came to that conclusion, I struggled whether or not to share my thoughts with anyone, especially with Mama and Addie. I could not sleep well that night as I tried to decide. By morning I had decided. There was no need to make anyone feel worse than they already felt. I kept my thoughts to myself.

"Moses," Paris said to me the next morning as we walked to the barn, " we need to have some man-to-man talks now that your

Papa is gone. Everythin's changed now. You're really too young to be a man, but that is what you gotta be now. Every day when we're workin' together, I am goin' to tell you some stories that I think you need to know and I'm goin' to share important advice so when the time is right, you will know everythin' you need to know. And, Moses, you will need your freedom stone; that stone has to guide your spirit."

Paris continued, "We are goin' to start right this minute. You have not heard the talk in the quarters, but the grownups talk about this story often, only in whispers, mind you." Paris continued.

"Many years ago, when I was still a young man, a slave named Nat Turner lived right here in this state of Virginia. He planned a rebellion against slave owners. He gathered together seventy slaves who were willing to carry out his plan.

"In the middle of the night, some on horseback, others running alongside, the mob went from house to house, freeing slaves and killing all the white people they came upon. In the end, about sixty men, women, and children were killed before the white militia defeated the angry slaves," Paris said.

I couldn't believe what I was hearing. "Paris, that's terrible! Sometimes I am angry, but I can't imagine wanting to kill someone."

Paris continued, "In the days that followed, the local militia and three artillery companies executed about two hundred black slaves in retribution. Fear spread throughout Virginia and the neighboring state of North Carolina. Such fear and alarm caused white people to attack blacks for any reason," Paris concluded. I just couldn't stand to hear that awful story. I grabbed Paris around the waist and I started to sob. I was thinking about James and Sarah. *I wouldn't dream of killing my good friends. And, sweet Missus. No, no, no, I couldn't do it. Never!*

"Son, I didn't tell you that story to frighten you. You need to know that tale because it made the white people terrified that their slaves might do the same thing to them. So, a lot of white people are now extra mean and cruel to try to keep us slaves in line."

I tried to imagine the slaves on the Porter Plantation rebelling. We were all frustrated about slavery, but I just couldn't see any of them, our friends, getting together to kill so many people.

"When I say that everythin' has changed, I meant that your Papa has died and you now need to be a man, but I also meant that things have changed for the white man too. Just need to understand it all, Moses."

"Yep, Paris, everythin's changed. I understand. I don't like it, but I understand. I am goin' to try to be more serious like Papa. I'm gonna try not to cry, ever. I'm gonna try to do what I now know I need to do," I said.

"Nothin' about trying, Moses. Can't just say you gonna try. Just say you are gonna do it," persuaded Paris.

"I promise, Paris. I will do it," I stammered.

"But, Moses, no one, absolutely no one, can know what you

are plannin'. Remember your father's words, 'eyes and ears open, mouth closed.'"

Everything was changed, including me. Something snapped when Papa died. Paris told me that I needed to be the man in the family now, and I knew that day that he was right. I wasn't sure that I had the courage, but I realized that I must be brave to do what I now knew that I had to.

Chapter Eight

A Big Surprise
July 1852

Addie

*"Now I've been free, I know what a dreadful
condition slavery is. I have seen hundreds of
escaped slaves, but I never saw one who was
willing to go back and be a slave."*

-Harriet Tubman

Bam! The back door slammed so hard, I almost felt the whole
house shake. I heard Massa screaming and hollering louder
than I had ever heard before.

I just had to find out what was going on.

Tiptoeing out of the kitchen and into the dining room, even though Mama was shaking her head 'no' at me, I hid behind the door where I could see and hear Massa carrying on.

With his back to me, Massa slammed that ol' Ben right down onto the hard, wooden bench right next to the door. The one where Massa and James sat to pull on their boots. Massa was shorter than Ben, but with Ben smacked down into the bench, Massa loomed over him. With their noses almost touching, Massa yelled, "What in the world were you thinking? Do you have a brain in that ugly head of yours?"

I couldn't believe what I was hearing.

"Dumb! Dumb! That was about the dumbest thing you have ever done! Your job here, the job I pay you for, is to oversee the slaves, not kill them!" Massa ranted.

Now they really had my attention. Massa was talking about Papa!

"I have half a mind to take that whip of yours and give you the same kind of welts on your back that you seem to delight in giving to the workers!" Massa continued.

"When a slave is ill, it is your job to let me know about it. Getting the work done is your job and don't you forget it! A sick slave cannot work as quickly or as efficiently as a healthy slave."

Ben just couldn't let that go. "Like the food you allow them is enough to keep them healthy!" he blurted.

I thought, *"I bet you are going to regret sassing Massa like that."*

"I'd fire you right now if it weren't getting so close to taking the tobacco to market. Let me tell you this, Ben Harrison, you do one more stupid thing like that and you will find out how mean and tough I can be! I'm probably going to have to buy another slave now. See how much you have cost me? And you are now one slave short to finish getting the tobacco ready for market!" Massa scolded.

I wanted Massa to beat Ben the same way Ben whipped Papa. Massa could beat Ben to death as far as I was concerned. I hated Massa when he hit Missus or James, but I was cheering him on when he punished Ben for the way he treated Papa. Go ahead, Massa. Hit him! Hit him!

Grabbing Ben by the front of his shirt, Massa pulled him up and threw him out into the yard.

Bam! That door slammed hard again.

Massa stomped off to his study, while I slipped back into the kitchen to tell Mama what I had witnessed. Mama got fiery angry. "I want Massa to do away with that awful man. No excuse for such an evil person. I wish he would….I wish he would….oh, I can't say, or I'd be evil too," she said.

Right soon after Papa died, Massa Porter decided that Moses should move into the big house with Mama and me. I thought maybe it was because he wanted to buy two more slaves, and he would put them in the cabin Moses had shared with Papa. Missus told me that it was because Mama needed him now since Papa wasn't around. What I really think is that Missus had a say about it.

Maybe she was protecting us from something. Maybe she thought that James and Moses would have more time to work on reading and numbers. Maybe she reckoned that she needed protection from something.

Every so often, I suspected that she had something up her sleeve that no one knew, just yet. No ifs, ands, or buts about that. She sure enough had something up her sleeve.

Whatever the reason, Moses brought his meager belongings over to the Big House and moved into the attic with Mama and me.

Moses said there were some good things about living in the big house, but there were some not so good things too.

It was nicer in the big house: he had a better bed to sleep on; he got to share in the leftovers when Mama cooked good breakfasts and dinners; he had more time to study with James; we children had more horsin' around time together; and he enjoyed Missus' company.

"But Addie, I miss 'em," he whispered to me one night when we couldn't get to sleep. "We were like a family in our cabin, helpin' each other through the hard times, and singin' and laughin' together when we could. Lafayette was a good story-teller; always encouraging us to be hopeful. I needed those big bear hugs Lizzie gave me. And baby Rachel - I loved to hold her on my lap and tickle her. I miss not having them around."

I was so glad to have Moses in the big house with us. It was sad losing Papa, and I needed the comfort of my brother. We often talked before falling asleep. His was the first face I saw in the morning, and he always greeted me with a quirky little smile, "Well, mornin' to ya, Adeline." (This was the only time he ever used my formal name). "Think it'll be a good mornin' or a bad mornin'?" He expected me to say that it would be a good mornin'. If I said, "Maybe it'll be a 'bad mornin',"" he told me to roll over and sleep a few more minutes until I could say it would be a good mornin'.

Living in the Big House meant Moses had to see and hear more of Massa. Mama and I had found ways to tolerate Massa's frequent outbursts. Some days he'd be all quiet-like and stay in his study with the big, heavy door closed. When he was like that, all in the house acted all quiet-like too. If one of us disturbed him, he might just bust loose out of there, yelling at anyone in his sight.

Some days he argued with Missus, though she tried to avoid that at all costs. But Moses was not used to all this yelling, and it made him uncomfortable.

Some evenings, Massa drank too much wine at dinner. He often picked a fight with Missus or James on those nights. Though Missus and James did everything they could to avoid getting into an argument with him, he couldn't be stopped.

One time, peeking around the kitchen door, I saw him rise

up out of his lordly chair and stomp down to the other end of the table and slap our beautiful Missus hard, right across her face. Some-how she steadied herself and with only a few tears slipping from her eyes, she touched her face with her hand, rose from the table and went up to her room.

By this time, James was up and furious. But, no surprise, he got his! Massa slapped him on the back of his head. This time James did not react. Sarah remained quiet, looking down at her lap.

Moses was beginning to learn about how to get along: keep your thoughts to yourself, say nothing, and nod when necessary. Just get along. One time I told him, "Moses, look at Mama and Missus and Sarah and me. We just lower our eyes and say nothin'. But watch James. He gets in trouble whenever he speaks up. Be careful," I warned. "Remember what Papa always said about your eyes and ears," I reminded him.

One day, just after breakfast, as Missus was helping Mama and me to clear the dishes from the table, she said, "Rebecca, I have a brilliant idea! William heads out for Richmond this after-noon to sell the tobacco. He'll be gone for at least three days, perhaps even four. It occurs to me that you and I, along with the children, deserve a small break from all of the goings-on around this place. My sister Abigail and her family live in Front Royal. They are always begging me to come for a visit. This is the perfect time. Don't you agree?"

"Oh, Mis' Martha. That sure enough is a grand idea! Want

me to go tell the other children?"

"No, Rebecca, this is our secret for now." Looking straight at me, Missus cautioned, "Adeline, you must keep it a secret too. Now, Rebecca, if you will pack a picnic lunch for the children and Paris, I will gather them around me and give them some instructions for the day…that is to say, I will get them out of the house and out of our hair so we can get ready for the trip." She turned to me, "Adeline, I want you to run to the barn and tell Moses that I need to see him here in the dining room."

"Yes'm," I agreed. I was so excited. I had never been off the plantation, and we were going to be with James and Sarah the whole time. I was already thinking about reading with Sarah on the trip. I ran so fast that I was surprised that I didn't trip over something on the way to the barn.

Out of breath and panting hard, I yelled as soon as I reached the doors of the barn, "Moses, Missus says come quick!'"

Immediately he dropped the pitchfork he was using to clean the stalls and joined me in a race back to the big house. I could tell that Moses was worried about the reason that Missus might need him right that minute. I'm sure he wondered what in the world was going on.

"What did I do, Addie?" he wheezed as he ran as fast as his legs would carry him.

"I don't think you did anythin' wrong, Moses, just hurry up," I answered. "Is Mama OK?" he asked.

"Yes, Mama's fine," I replied.

99

When Missus saw the frightened look on Moses' face, she laughed. "My goodness, Moses, you look as if you have just seen a ghost! Why are you so jittery?"

"Well, I thought something pretty awful must have happened," he said.

Missus gathered us in her arms and gave us a big squeeze. "No, no, no," she went on, "I have a plan for today and I want to tell you about it. But before I do, please fetch James and Sarah also, because they are a part of the plan too."

When all four of us were huddled together, Mistress told us about her plan. "Rebecca and I need a little privacy today, so, James, Sarah, and Adeline, I want all of you to go to work in the barn with Moses and Paris. With so many hands to do the work, there should be time for a little play too. Or perhaps Paris can tell you one of his best stories. Rebecca has prepared a scrumptious picnic lunch for all of you. You must do the work that Moses and Paris complete in a day, but as soon as you have done that you may spend the day as you like. But I do not want to see your faces in this house until dinner. Everybody understand?"

Nodding our heads all at the same time, James and Moses cleared out of there as quick as a flash, leaving us girls struggling with the heavy basket filled with the delicious food that Mama had prepared for us.

After dinner, which all of us enjoyed at the great dining room table, (What a special occasion for Moses, Mama and me to actually sit down at the big table in the dining room!), Mistress confessed that she and Mama had decided to take us on a trip to visit Missus' sister in Front Royal. Though it was only going to be a trip of about forty-five miles, Moses and I were plenty excited. Moses had been into Culpeper a few times with James or with Paris, but he had never been that far away from the plantation. The trip was going to be a first for me.

It was mighty hard to go to sleep that night thinking about what lay ahead of us the next morning. Mama finally had to sing soothing African lullaby tunes to get us calmed down enough to fall asleep.

Mama and Missus awakened us before daylight.

"James, go out to the barn and hitch up Thunder and Old Tom to the large carriage and bring it around out front," instructed Missus. "And, Moses, go tell Paris so he won't worry about you, but warn him that I do not want him mentioning it to any of the others, not even to Lafayette and Lizzie," Missus added.

James drove the carriage with Missus sitting at his side. The rest of us sat in the back, squeezed together tighter than newborn baby birds in a nest.

I cannot remember seeing my Mama with such a joyful,

peaceful look on her face, and was she ever singing! Mama sometimes hummed along with Papa, but I had never heard her sing so beautifully. She even taught all of us some African tunes that we had not heard before…funny sounding words, but what rhythm! We clapped and sang happily as we bumped along toward Front Royal.

We stopped a few times for the horses to sip some clear, cool water from a stream and for us to take a necessary run into the woods. But we got back on our way quickly; seemed like Missus did not want to waste any time getting to see her sister.

Just when my stomach was starting to tell me that it was lunch time, Missus asked James to bring the carriage to a stop at Catlett Creek, about half way to Front Royal. Settling the horses at the creek and putting out a feedbag of oats for them, James did as he was told.

Mama laid out a large white cloth on the ground and we all dug into that picnic lunch of dried beef, Mama's famous biscuits, sliced tomatoes, green beans with ham hock, and peaches.

I never ate so good!

Then Missus went and dropped a cannonball on us! I thought this trip was the big surprise, but I had no idea what was coming up next…

Missus started, "I am going to let you all in on a big secret." She got all choked up and teary-eyed, but she continued, "This day will be the beginning of Rebecca's, Adeline's, and Moses' passage to freedom."

Really crying pretty good now, she told us that on that very day we would run away.

Run away.

She said the words, 'Run away.'

For a few moments, none of us knew what to say. It was so quiet that you could hear Thunder and Old Tom chompin' on their oats. I could hear our breaths.

Mama was the first to speak; by now she was crying too. "Missus, you would do that for us?"

"Of course, Rebecca. It is the right thing to do. There is no reason why your family should not be as free as mine. I cannot put my head down on the pillow at night if I don't help you to find a way to escape this terrible condition called slavery. You know that I have always tried to treat everyone fairly. I keep hoping that slavery will end soon. But after your husband died in such an unforgiveable way, I could no longer sit by and watch you live as slaves. I knew I needed to do something."

By then all of us were sobbing, hugging each other, and even nervously giggling some too.

Missus continued, "Maybe one day all slaves will be free. I would work for that myself, but you know the life I must lead at the plantation. I have to think about James and Sarah and what might happen to us if William ever found out how I really feel about slavery. In my heart, I cannot find a way to justify buying people the same way you might buy a horse or a mule. I think it is wrong to expect people to work long hours for no pay so that the slave owner can make more money. And, it gives me great pain to stand by and watch how badly slaves are treated by Ben at the direction of my husband."

"So this is the most I can do for now…help you whom I consider to be my family, my dear family.

"Now I know that you all have heard stories about slaves who tried to run away and were caught and returned to their masters. But I want you to know that some runaway slaves have escaped and found their freedom. One slave who did that was a woman named Harriet Tubman, and after she found her freedom she came back again and again, helping others to be free," Missus added.

With some power inside of herself, Missus got us all to stop sobbing so she could finish her instructions.

"Moses, I expect you to be the leader on this journey North. You must travel mostly at night and hide during the day so that the slave catchers and the patrollers won't find you. You know what will happen to you if they do. James, please fetch those things that I had you put into the carriage before we left home."

James presented Moses with a knife, a flint, some lengths of rope, and a small fishing net.

Missus could tell that Moses was scared and confused, but she looked him straight in the eye and said seriously, "You may need to kill a squirrel or a rabbit to eat. You may need to catch some fish. Take care not to lose these tools. They may be your lifeline.

"And Moses, it's natural to be afraid doing what you are about to do. We're all afraid sometimes; I'm afraid right now too. But bravery is doing what you have to do, even when you are terribly afraid. And I know in my heart that you are brave."

Missus put the leftovers from our lunch in a small cloth, tied the corners together, and handed it to Mama.

My emotions were getting the best of me. I was trembling. I grabbed my friend Sarah and hugged her with all my might. I tried to say something to her, but my words got jumbled up with my crying. Moses and James were locked in a big hug too. Mama and Missus seemed to be inseparable.

We were all crying. Missus got her wits about her and gave us instructions. "Find a good hiding place until it gets dark, then follow the creek until it slows to a trickle. At that point, go straight into the woods for about as many steps as it was from your cabin to the barn. Head north following the North Star until you see a small white farmhouse with a lantern shining on the front stoop. This will be your first safe house, your first station on the Underground Railroad. Knock on the back door. You will be greeted warmly."

"Now run!"

CHAPTER NINE

Runaways
October 1852

Moses

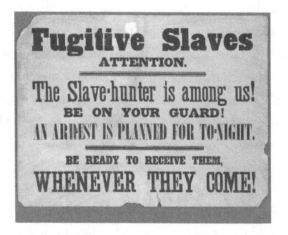

"Now, run! That's what Missus said. Go that way," I told Mama and Addie, pointing the way. I took off, running as if I were in a race. There was no distinct path; we had to make our own, tripping over tree roots and briers. When I passed Mama and Addie, I could hear them panting as they ran. We were all out of breath.

"Let's stop for a minute," I said.

I had dreamed of the day when I would be able to escape. I had thought about ways I might do it. Above all, I had decided that, unlike many other runaway slaves who ran away by themselves, I just had to take Mama and Addie with me.

Yes, I'd given it a lot of thought. All of us in the quarters thought about it constantly, and Paris and I talked about it many times when we knew there was no one else around to hear our conversation.

But there was one big thing that I had not thought about. And that was how I would feel leaving Missus, James and Sarah. Standing there watching their wagon slowly disappear in the distance, I wanted to cry. Missus had always been so kind. She was the one who wanted Addie and me to learn to read and write. She was the one who always complimented Mama's cooking.

James and Sarah were positively our best friends. I could not imagine what our lives would be like without them. My thoughts ran to our community of slaves; we were a family. How could I possibly leave, never to know what might happen to each of them?

These thoughts were still whirling about inside my head when I realized that I had lost sight of the wagon entirely.

Suddenly new thoughts took their place.

The gruesome whippings endured by most of Massa's slaves, usually occurring for no good reason. The welts on Paris' back. Paris wailing his wife's name as he was beaten. Papa dying because he couldn't do the strenuous work required of him, even when he was sick. Ben riding around on his horse with his whip in his hand, ready to use if he just felt like it. Winter days when our clothing was too thin to keep us or warm or the summer days, when we couldn't take a break when it was so hot and we couldn't see straight because the sweat was pouring into our eyes. Massa's constant yelling, calling us every nasty name that anyone ever heard of. The story of my own mother standing on an auction block, being sold to the highest bidder…a human being sold…just like a wagon, a horse, tobacco, or farm equipment.

Flashing before my eyes was the word 'property'.

We were someone's property.

When I could not get that word out of my mind, I knew that I had to do whatever it took for the three of us to find our freedom.

But I was paralyzed. My legs felt like tree trunks with roots deep in the ground. I was unable to move.

Suddenly, the words came back to me, "Bravery is doing what you have to do even when you are terribly afraid." I was so scared that I could hardly breathe, but I kept my hand on that stone in my pocket, rubbing my fingers back and forth across the sharp point at one end.

And then, I figured it out! The point on my freedom stone was a symbol. It was a sign telling me to go north.

Missus had given us a head start. We would not be considered missing until Missus, James and Sarah returned from Front Royal without us. The slave catchers would not be called for a few days. What a gift Missus gave us!

Now we were alone.

We were close enough to the stream to see the water, but far enough away from it so that we would not be easily seen. We walked for a long time while I gathered my thoughts and figured out a plan.

Spotting a massive, fallen chestnut tree a little deeper in the woods, I led Mama and Addie to it. We crouched together, hidden in its large branches, sipped from our water gourds, and discussed our strategy.

"Let's keep going now. I'm not tired yet. We need to run. That's what Missus said, '"Run,"' Addie suggested. Mama took a deep breath, and sighed, "Well, I don't know about you, girl, but I, for one, am very tired." I disagreed with Addie. "Yes, Missus did say that, but, Addie, you seem to have forgotten that we've been taught that it's smarter to hide and sleep during the day and run at night when we won't be seen," I countered. "Moses, you think you're so smart! Don't forget, I'm two years older than you. Nobody sleeps during the day!" Addie was really getting agitated. "Don't be so sassy," I snapped back.

Right away, I realized that I was being childish. I could almost hear Paris' voice,'" Your Papa has died, and now you need to be a man."' So, I continued, as calmly as I could, - inside I wasn't very calm at all - "Here's our plan. We'll keep running for a little while, until Mama gets too tired. Then we're going to need to find another shelter as good as this big tree, so we can hide and get some sleep."

I explained to Mama and Addie about what Paris had taught me about walking quietly in the woods. He told me that the Monacan Indians who lived in our part of Virginia knew how to walk just softly enough that the noise of their footsteps was quieter than the normal commotion in the woods, softer than the wind blowing through the branches of the trees, tree branches breaking and falling, animal sounds, and birds chirping. "We need to walk so that our feet touch the ground at the same time," I instructed. "That way there is only the sound of one foot, not three."

Mama said, "We should try to cover our footsteps as we push through the underbrush and thickets."

"Good idea, Mama," Addie agreed. I told Mama and Addie, "The last person in our line of three can grab small twigs and branches and throw them behind after each step. Addie, you and Mama take turns being the last in line. I will go first and make the path." I thought Addie might argue with me about my plan, but she, like I, had decided that we better work together, or we'd never find freedom.

We devised a plan so that we could communicate if it was necessary. We would use stones to bang against our water gourds. Hitting the gourd one time meant that it was clear and safe ahead. Two strikes against the gourd gave the message to hide and to be very still, as danger was nearby. If one of us was hurt, or in any other kind of serious trouble, three smacks on the gourd meant, "Come help me!" When we hit the stone against the gourd, we planned to wait a short time and then repeat the call. We knew we could not talk loudly or call out to each other, under any circumstances.

We ran for a while longer, but when I spied another uprooted tree that would give us shelter, we stopped to sleep. When it turned dark, Mama woke Addie and me. We shared a bite of our food, trying to conserve some as long as possible.

Heading back toward the creek, we resumed our journey. We moved quickly even running some of the time. The moon was bright and I was confident that we were moving northward.

Suddenly, I heard the sounds of horses' hooves coming toward us!

We had to find a place to hide!

There was no time.

I was shaking. My heart was pounding so fast that I could hardly breathe. *What are we goin' to do? It sounds like more than one horse. How are we goin' to get out of this? I can tell by the looks on their faces; Mama and Addie are scared too. Think! Think, Moses. You're supposed to be the leader.*

Knowing Papa would want me to take care of Mama and Addie, I rushed to the water, where I found two black willows leaning into the water. I directed Mama and Addie with my eyes and a nod. We slid noiselessly into the water hiding ourselves among the draping branches. The water was deep there. It was resting at my hips…Mama and Addie were in the creek above their waists. Mama hoisted the cloth containing what little was left of our food onto a branch above her head and was busy tying it to the branch when Addie whispered, "The cloth is white! It can be seen!" Mama nodded and quickly removed it and stuck it inside her blouse.

Louder and louder came the sound of the hooves.

Closer and closer.

We could hear voices.

Why, oh why, did they decide to stop so near to us?

There were two of them, both with guns at their sides.

One man started a fire in a small clearing about thirty paces from us. The other led the two horses to the water just steps from where we were hiding. I don't think the three of us took a single breath while the horses drank from the cool creek. Though the water was cold, I was sweating. My knees felt weak and I thought I might throw up.

Sitting by their fire, the two men cooked whatever food they had brought with them, opened a bottle of some stuff that I guessed was what people called Virginia lightning. They ate and drank and talked about an escaped slave named Demetry Field. We could hear bits and pieces of their conversation, especially after they had a little more to drink and their voices got a little louder. The slave had been missing for nearly a week and had run away from the Field Plantation in Little Falls. The reward for catching the slave was $200. That was a large sum of money. That slave must have been valuable to his slave owner. These two slave catchers were certain that they were going to catch the slave and share the reward. They were already laughing and talking about how they would spend that money.

The water was freezing. My legs were stiff and my feet were numb.

The men took their bed rolls from the backs of the horses and proceeded to lie down and go to sleep!

We could not move until they woke up. We were stuck right where we were for many hours. The silence made my blood run cold. My heart raced so fast, it sounded like a drum.

With the dawn, the two men wakened, stoked the fire and fixed themselves something to eat. They shoveled their food into their mouths, not even talking to each other. Bringing their horses to the water once again, they were close enough that we could see their faces as they filled their water canteens. I don't think I had ever seen such dirty looking men. They must have been riding for days. They were not close enough for me to smell them, but they must have reeked. Their clothes were dirty and one of them had half of one of his pant-legs torn off. Their squinty eyes and ugly scowls would have frightened the devil!

One of the men said to the other with a disgusting snort, "Let's go get that pitiful slave." I shuddered when they laughed, as they mounted the horses and were on their way at a pretty fast pace.

Stumbling out of the water, we attempted to get our legs

working right again.

Addie started to cry. "I don't think that I can go through with this," she sobbed. "We barely made it through this night; who knows what the next days will bring? I think we should go back."

Mama responded quickly, almost hissing at Addie, "No, we will not go back! You know what would happen to us if we did? We would all be whipped within an inch of our lives, and it wouldn't end there! It would continue over and over again over any little thing that Ben or Massa decided that they didn't like."

"Addie, no! We are not goin' back. We can't give up now. You don't know how terrible it can be! I have wanted to spare you from the awful things I endured. I never wanted to tell you before, but now you must know. We are runaways now. We are goin' to be free!"

Mama started weeping and shaking. She could hardly catch her breath. Even when Papa died, she didn't sob like this, jumping up and down, her head bobbing from one shoulder to the other. Her wet clothes sloshing around her, Mama started to moan, but Addie quieted her immediately. "Mama, Mama, ssh....ssh....we can't let anyone hear us."

Mama quieted down, but spoke through clenched teeth in an angry whisper. "I can shut my eyes and I see everythin'! Everythin'! I can see everythin'! I can see the tears runnin' down my mama's face when the slave catchers put chains on my ankles and dragged me away from my town! I can see the angry, sad,

115

and tired eyes of all of the other children walkin' slowly along with me on our march to the sea! I can see the insides of the horrid, windowless dungeon where we were kept for days waitin' for the arrival of the ship that would take us to America! I cannot ever forget what it felt like to be dragged up the gangplank on that awful ship and then bein' pulled down to the cargo hold, where we were chained and crammed together for the months that it took to cross the ocean!"

Mama was going on like a maniac. The thought entered my mind that she had gone insane. Addie and I tried to calm her, but she would have none of it.

On and on and on she ranted, occasionally raising her voice. "Mama, remember to keep your voice low," reminded Addie. Mama was spilling out years and years of memories that she had hidden from us.

I was still worried that someone might hear, but there was no stopping her.

"I can smell the stench from our own waste! I can smell the dead bodies of some who never made it off the ship!"

"Mama, more softly, please," I begged.

"My legs feel like they could crumble beneath me right now, just as they did when at last the ship arrived in America and I tried to walk after havin' been chained up for so long! I can feel the sliminess of the oil they spread all over my skin to make me look healthy. I can see every one of those nasty, evil men draggin' me from the slave pen up onto that auction block in front of all those white folks buyin' up us slaves. Those rotten slave bidders treated me just the same as if they had been buyin' a horse or a pig. Made me strip! Poked and pinched me all over, made me bend this way and that! Even stuck their hands in my mouth to look at my teeth. Yes, I can see everythin.'"

Mama's madness finally wore her out and she fell to the ground wracked with sobs.

Stroking her face calmly, Addie cradled Mama's head against her shoulder and she began to sing one of Mama's favorite songs.

Swing low, sweet chariot,
Coming for to carry me home,
Swing low, sweet chariot,
Coming for to carry me home.

Mama gave Addie and me a big hug, and began an attempt to wring out her clothes. We had no other clothes, so we would have to let them dry while we were in them.

I told Addie and Mama that since I had felt fish swimming around my legs all night in the stream, I might just as well go catch one for our breakfast since we had a fire right there waiting for us to use it.

I headed back to our hiding tree and leaned down over the water with the fishing net in my hand. I lowered my arm into the water as far as it would go without falling head over heels into the water, and I pretended that those two men were still there so that I could be as still as I had been during the night. I held my arm that way for a long time until I thought it would fall right off; then I felt it.

Must be a pretty good-sized one at that.

I whipped my arm up so fast, just like Paris taught me, that I frightened Mama who seemed about to jump out of her skin.

"Mama, I got us a nice trout for our breakfast! Are there any biscuits left?

CHAPTER TEN

Injury Slows Us Down
October 1852

Addie

The heaviness of our wet clothes made walking more difficult and slow. We certainly did not relish the thought of lying down in wet clothes either, but we were exhausted from being awake all night. We trudged along, daring to be a little closer to the water where there were fewer trees and more sunshine. With good luck, we did not see anyone nor did we think we were seen.

Shortly after noon, I found a spacious depression in the ground with a heavy stand of thicket and underbrush almost surrounding it...a soft sleeping place, its only disadvantage, damp earth. With no other choices, we settled in.

Moses and Mama fell asleep quickly, while I worried about where our next meal might come from. It had been several hours since our breakfast, and we had no more food.

Mama had always been clever in finding wild grapes, huckle-berries, and blackberries in the woods. My hope was that she would have some luck in the coming days finding some for us to eat. I was pretty sure that Moses could catch another fish, but this time he would need to make a fire. Most all the time we had a fire going in the quarters, but I wasn't sure whether Moses was ever the person who started it. I hoped that he would remember how to do it, but I had started all the fires in the Big House, so I knew I could help. I think I dozed for a short while.

With only a few hours of daylight left, Moses woke up and sought out a good fishing spot where he could see water movement around some weeds hanging into the water. He tried and tried, but this time his net was empty.

Awake now, Mama reassured me that we would find some berries. We filled our water gourds and resumed our journey.

By the end of the second day, we had eaten all our food. Moses tried to kill a squirrel with his knife, but he missed. He tried to catch another fish, but the water was running so swiftly that he kept losing his footing and he fell into the water many times. I know he was discouraged.

Though Missus had not said how far it would be before the creek narrowed to a trickle, we assumed that it would not be very far, so we were discouraged as we noticed the creek widen on our fourth day. How long would we have to run before we found a safe house?

I am tired and weary but I must toil on,
Til the Lord come to call me away.

Nothing to eat.
Nothing to eat.
There was no moon that night, which probably was a good thing because we had to be so focused on going in the direction. We had no time to mope about our growling stomachs.

We were all worried about whether or not we were going north. With no light to guide us, we had to follow as Moses led us along the edge of the creek. When we got close enough, we could catch a glimpse now and then of the ripples in the water. More than a few times, we found ourselves in the water after tripping on a tree root or a large rock. Falling into the creek might have been funny any other time, but all I could think of

121

was how afraid we were and that we were miserable in our cold, wet clothes.

The land was getting steeper and steeper. We knew that the mountains lay north of Culpeper, so that gave us some assurance that we were heading north.

One of the times that Moses tumbled into the water, he decided to give fishing another try. There were several large rocks both in the water and on the shore. I managed to find two large rocks in the woods and using every ounce of strength we had, Moses and I were able to push them into the water near a small rapids.

We created a narrow opening through which we hoped at least one fish might swim. Perilously perched atop our little reef, Moses leaned over and jammed his fishing net between the two rocks.

We waited and waited for what seemed like forever, and then Moses raised that net high as quickly as he could, just as he tumbled over the rocks into the water. Though he was falling, there was no way on the earth that he was going to let that fish get away.

Somehow, he gave that net a huge toss toward me. I tried to catch it, but I missed. The fish fell on the ground, free of the net.

Moses scrambled out of the water, grabbing the fish and jamming it back into the net.

Moses wasn't seriously hurt, but he hid have a few bangs and bruises here and there. Though his pride suffered some damage, we were mighty glad to have the fish! When daylight came around, we would be able to make a fire and have something to eat.

The weather had not yet turned cold, but we were freezing anyway in our damp clothes. We knew that continually wearing wet clothes was probably not good for us, but we couldn't do a thing about it. To keep our minds off our discomfort, we decided that we should practice the Indian way of stepping in unison for as long as we could.

The sky was beginning to brighten and we were finally able to see our way a little bit better. Our steps hit the ground at the same time and we made a little game of it.

I suggested that we try to keep it up until we reached the drooping river birch just ahead. When we got there, I challenged us to keep going the Indian way until we saw a bear. Mama and Moses thought my idea was quite preposterous because of course we hoped we would not ever see a bear on our journey. The challenge kept us moving along at a snail's pace for a long time. We didn't like going so slow because it meant that the trip would take longer, putting us at a greater risk of being caught. Keeping quiet was more important than going faster, so we kept walking Indian-style.

Dawn soon became full daylight, and again we had to find a resting place. I volunteered to find a new hiding spot for us while Mama stepped out to find some berries.

Moses told me that he was going to find a small clearing where he could get a fire going, first gathering dry grasses and seedpods and putting them together to form a small mound. Later he could strike his knife along the edge of the flint that James had given him.

I took off, scouting around for some ripe berries that we could add to our fish dinner. At the same time, I was searching for another good, dry hiding spot where we could sleep for at least a few hours.

But I wasn't looking where I was going...looking forward, not down where my feet were.

I stepped into a hole and tumbled to the ground, hitting my head on a tree stump. I hadn't knocked myself out cold, but I was dizzy. My head was pounding; I had such a bad headache. My hands flew to my sore head before I realized that my foot was stuck. I had to use both hands to pry it loose. I couldn't tell if it was my foot or my ankle. All I knew was that it hurt. Worse than my head hurt. It really hurt.

Grabbing a stone, I hit my drinking gourd, hard, three times. I waited a few more seconds. Three powerful hits again. I did this about four times, hoping that Mama and Moses would hear my call for help. When they didn't come, I started all over again banging on my gourd as hard as I could.

Three times.

Wait.

Three more times.

By the time Mama and Moses found me, I was crying as quietly as I could. I did not want anyone to hear me. I was still lying in a heap on the ground.

My ankle was swelling quickly and Mama worried, "I think she broke it!"

"Mama, I will be fine after I rest; we are gettin' closer. I just sense it!"

Mama propped a small log atop another so that I could elevate my foot. Moses ran back to dip his shirt into the water to make a wrap for my ankle. On the way, he checked on the fire and the fish. The fire had gone out, but even so, he threw the fish onto the coals.

Moses and Mama were able to get me comfortably settled among the branches on the ground.

Moses went back to get the fish, which surprisingly had become quite a nice smoked treat for our breakfast, along with the huckleberries that Mama had found.

Moses and Mama fell asleep, while I worried about how we might get along with my injury. I must have fallen asleep because when I wakened it was dark, but the sky was beautiful with a full moon and millions of stars. I decided that it was a good sign.

Walking was extremely difficult and painful. Mama and Moses each took one side and draped my arms around their shoulders so I wouldn't have to put my weight on the sore ankle. I hopped along on my good foot. Progress was slow as we had to stop often for all of us to rest.

While resting, I suggested, "I think we should find two strong branches that I can use like crutches."

"What a great idea!" Mama replied. And quick as a wink, Moses was off to find crutches for me. Though they were heavy to handle, I did surprisingly well with the tree-crutches Moses found.

Hours passed, but we were moving quite efficiently, if slowly, considering my condition.

Suddenly I noticed something that we had been searching for: "Look," I said. "The water has slowed to a trickle! We must be near our first station on the underground railroad!"

We three had never been as happy as we were in that moment.

Moses worried, "I might have forgotten how many steps it was from the slave quarters to the barn." But as he led us straight into the woods, his confidence seemed to return.

When we reached the spot where we felt we should turn north, Moses searched for the North Star. Taking that stone out his pocket, he instructed each of us to rub it over and over again, hoping it would be a good luck charm. Finding the star, we stumbled northward until I had to stop.

"I can't stand the pain any longer. I have to give up. You two go ahead."

"We are not givin' up! Addie, have you forgotten all of the things I told you? Those are the reasons why we must find our freedom; I am not goin' to let you forget them now. You can't ever forget what happened to me, hear? Moses and I will carry you in our arms until we find the safe house. Now let's get goin'!"

Mama admonished.

Together, Mama and Moses made a fourhanded seat for me and carried me like that until I was sure their backs would break. We had to stop many times that night so that we could all rest. Mama and Moses were exhausted from carrying me, and I was in so much pain that I wasn't sure that I could keep going. Our progress, therefore, was slowed to a turtle's pace.

Desperately trying to stay awake for nighttime travel, there were three or four times we gave in to our weariness and napped for short times. Each time we awakened, they gathered me in their arms and shuffled along for as long a stretch as we could endure.

The morning sun alerted us to find a quiet spot. We understood that we had not journeyed far during the evening so we dared to keep moving at the risk of being seen.

Starting and stopping.

Starting and stopping.

Such was the way of our parade through the woods. I knew how hungry we all were, but we focused on the trail and kept moving forward. We spent the daylight hours weary and ready to drop at any moment.

As late afternoon began to show signs of turning to dusk, we stumbled upon a large, fallen pine where we decided to pause for a few hours.

Early that evening I told Mama and Moses that I thought I could walk with my arms draped around their shoulders again,

127

so we could move a little faster. "Are you sure, Addie?" Mama inquired. "I don't want you to damage that ankle any worse than it already is."

I replied, "I will not let my bad foot touch the ground; I will keep my weight on the good leg and your shoulders. But I am starvin', and I have no water left in my water gourd."

Giving the last drop of the water in his gourd to me, Moses led us on our stumbling march north.

Hungry.

So hungry.

I made up a silly jingle so that we walked in a bit of rhythm… left foot, left foot, go ahead, go ahead, walk 'til we find that house. We had not gone far when we thought we spotted a light in the distance. Could it be the lantern on the farmhouse?

Chapter Eleven

Danger! Hide!
October 1852

Moses

*"There is not a man beneath the
canopy of Heaven who does not
know that slavery is wrong for him."*

-*Frederick Douglass*

"Oh, my poor dears, come in, come in! You look so weary."
A kind-looking short, plump woman welcomed us
immediately. Standing next to her was her husband, a towering
robust figure, who picked Addie up the second he spotted her

sore ankle. As he gently set her down in a comfortable chair, he propped up her leg with many cushions, and asked, "Child, what happened to you?" Somehow Addie got the gift of a rippling tongue and explained in great detail how she had hurt herself, throwing in a few other parts of our story for good measure.

"Husband, these dear folks do not yet know us. How can they feel certain at this moment that they can trust us?" the good-hearted woman interrupted.

I of course was wondering about that very thing, as Papa and others in the slave quarters had warned us over and over again about telling white people stories that might get another slave in trouble.

Addie had completely forgotten Papa's instructions.

"Let us introduce ourselves," the lady continued.

"My husband is Jacob Harlan and I am Lydia Harlan. We are called abolitionists. We are Quakers, and Quakers believe that slavery is wrong. We are trying to do our part to help slaves on their journey to freedom.

"Not all abolitionists are white Quakers. Some are free black people. Frederick Douglass is an important man whose work you may know about. Douglass was a slave in Maryland before he escaped. Once a free man, he began to tell his story to anyone who would listen. He is a great man, well-respected by many in the abolitionist cause," Lydia finished.

"You are welcome here in our home," Jacob said. "We will help in any way that we are able, but we must all be careful and prepare for the possible search of our home and barn by patrollers or slave catchers. We have not had three runaways in our home at the same time, so your sleeping arrangements will be quite small and perhaps not as comfortable as we would like, but we will keep you safe. Please feel free to call us by our first names.

"Lydia and I have a small daughter named Elise, who is just learning to walk. You can help us to keep her occupied; we will appreciate the extra hands," Jacob said.

"We have a small farm which supplies our basic food needs, but we also have an apple orchard. We take our apples to market in September and October, so you are here at a good time. I'm sure that you will be here for several days while that ankle heals, so we will get to know each other as we work together and share meals.

"Now, why don't you tell us about yourselves?"

Mama and I were still a little reserved about spilling too much information. Addie did not seem to have any such reservations. We each took turns telling the Harlans about our lives on the Porter Plantation and about how Missus had helped us to start on our runaway path.

Patting Addie warmly and sympathetically on her shoulder, Jacob told us that he believed that Addie's ankle was indeed broken and that we would need a doctor to reset the bone.

"Finding a doctor who will treat a runaway slave would be a risky undertaking," Jacob said. "We'll have to settle for a bonesetter. I have a friend who supports our efforts to help runaway slaves. He is pretty good at setting the broken bones of our farm animals; I will ride to his farm tomorrow morning and ask for his help."

Mama made friends with Elise immediately. She got down on the floor, and played a peek-a-boo game, covering her eyes with both hands. She opened her arms wide and said, "Peek-a-boo, I see you." Elise started giggling. Mama smiled for the first time in a long time; I could see her beginning to relax.

Lydia served us a hearty vegetable soup and some biscuits that tasted almost as good as Mama's. What followed was a long and serious discussion about what we had to know to stay safe.

Jacob took Mama and me upstairs to show us where we would sleep. To get to our sleeping space, he pushed a heavy dresser aside revealing a small opening in the wall covered with a piece of wood that served as a wee door. When I got down on my knees and peeked in, I saw a cramped space created by the sloping roof and the floor of one of the bedrooms. A triangular area with floor space measuring about 2 ½ feet wide and a short wall of about 3 ½ feet height would be our sleeping spot. The roof sloped down steeply so that at one side it was only about six inches high. Once inside the humble under-eave space, we noticed there were two straw mattresses placed end-to-end; Mama and Addie would have to share a bed.

Though Jacob was apologetic about the size of the area and its lack of comfort, we assured him that it was more comfortable than anything we were used to.

"Now, remember, if we sense danger coming during the day and if we have enough time, we will hide you in this space and you will have to remain here until we believe that danger has passed," Jacob warned. "If we do not have enough time to get up here, we have three other hiding places on our property. We will show those to you tomorrow after you have had some rest."

Jacob turned to his wife, "Lydia, dear, can you find some clean, dry clothes for our guests?"

We followed Lydia out to the barn where there was a small storage room at one end. Here Jacob kept a small pony cart, a hand plow, and a collection of various farm implements. I am guessing, but I think the room was about 8 feet by 8 feet. Lydia had a surprise for us. "Moses, come here and help me, son." She moved the pony cart and pointed toward the floor. Near the bottom of the wall and attached to it was a metal handle. "See that handle, Moses? Give it a good tug. But, be careful, step back quickly as you pull or you will knock yourself out." I gave it a try. The whole wall lifted right out and up! It was a secret door. Mama laughed. Addie gasped. I just stood there; I was so shocked. Clothing items of all sizes filled the secret room. Lydia asked us to help her search through the britches, shirts, dresses, hats, and shoes to find things that would fit each of us. I still had a perplexed look on my face. She asked me, "What's wrong, Moses?"

"Nothin'," I replied. "Just wonderin' where you got all this stuff."

"Many of our abolitionist friends collect and donate these things to us. They want to play a part in the Underground Railroad, even if they cannot open their homes to runaways."

It was a new experience for us to select our own clothes. We were so grateful to get out of the damp clothes that had been sticking to our skin for so many days.

And our shoes. Our feet had been soaked for so long that the skin was soft and shriveled up like a prune.

We had blisters and more blisters. Lydia washed and dried our feet. She put some soothing salve on our feet, finishing with clean dry socks and shoes. Such a loving gesture.

Jacob carried Addie upstairs and we settled in, falling asleep almost immediately. Knowing that the dresser was pushed back over the opening to our small cubby, we were confident that we were safe.

We wakened the next morning when we heard Lydia cooing and singing to Elise just outside our wall. The dresser had been moved and we were able to squeeze out into the daylight.

Elise was delighted to see us; Addie played with her while Lydia, Mama and I shoved the furniture back over the opening.

Addie slid down the stairs on her bottom. Elise thought it was funny so she tried to copy Addie. She needed a little help from Mama as her legs were too short to slide from one step to the next. Elise's attempts at bumping down the steps on her bottom made Addie smile...a big, broad smile. I hadn't seen that in a good, long while! *Now, they're both smiling...Addie and*

Mama. Things are lookin' up.

Once we were all gathered in the kitchen, we noticed that Jacob had left on his horse to seek the help of his friend, the bonesetter.

"You know Lydia, I was a cook at the plantation and I sure know how to wring a chicken's neck, gather eggs, and smoke pork. And I must say that I make mighty good biscuits and pies. I cleaned their house, and washed and ironed the clothes, so I hope you will let me help you," Mama offered.

"Rebecca, thank you! How about some of those biscuits for our breakfast? We'll serve them with the strawberry jam I made last spring.

Addie and Elise were chasing each other around the kitchen table. Not much of a chase, really. Elise was so tiny; she had just learned to walk. And, Addie's ankle hurt her so bad, she barely hobbled about. But they were having fun playing this little game while I waited for some instruction from Lydia as to how I could help out. "Elise seems to be quite taken with you, Addie; will you play with her while we whip up some breakfast?" Lydia helped Addie and Elise to a big rocking chair in the main room on the first floor of the house. Handing Addie a child's book, she suggested, "Why don't you read to Elise?" As soon as the words slipped from her mouth, she said, "Oh Addie, I'm sorry. I forgot that you probably don't read."

"But I do," answered Addie right away. "I do know how to read. Missus taught me."

"Wonderful," Lydia said. "Now, Moses, will you sweep the front porch? Maybe Jacob will be home soon to join us," Lydia said.

Jacob arrived home in time for breakfast along with his friend, Mr. Samuel Burk, a big strong man with a kind smile. Mr. Burk looked like he could wrestle with a bull, yet treat the bull with the respect he deserved. I immediately liked him before he had even spoken a word. I just had a good feeling about him.

Sitting at a table for breakfast was still a relatively new experience for my family and we enjoyed it. But what came next was not quite so pleasant.

Mr. Burk had a look at Addie's ankle and declared it broken. Laying Addie on top of the breakfast table, he tugged and pulled on Addie's leg. He pushed and pulled on that ankle until he was assured that the bone was back in place as close as he could get it.

Addie was in such terrible pain that she shrieked loudly, scaring Elise who started to wail herself. Lydia gave Addie a thick cloth with the suggestion that she bite on it to help her to deal with the agony; that seemed to help.

Mr. Burk wrapped the ankle tightly, advising Addie not to put her weight on that leg for two weeks. He gave her a pair of crutches and told her to keep it elevated as much of the day as possible. "Go down to the trout stream at the foot of the hill and cool your unwrapped ankle in the stream at least once every day. And, giving Addie a big hug, he said, "You are one very brave girl."

"So, you are stuck with us for at least two weeks," Jacob laughed. "Do you think you can stand it?"

"We are very content to stay here for a few weeks," Mama said. "You are such a kind family and I feel that we are welcome here. Missus told us so when she sent us on our way to your home. But I am worried about you. With us in your house for such a long time, we are putting your lives in danger."

"Rebecca, thank you for your concern. Jacob and I accept the risk that we take when trying to help runaways. We believe it is an obligation to care for one another," Lydia said, patting Mama's hand.

Jacob continued our safety discussion from the night before, warning us that patrollers or slave catchers could show up at any time and they had the right, by law, to search the entire property if they suspected that there were hidden runaways.

Three additional hiding places existed on the Harlan farm: one more inside the house, one in the barn, and one in the apple orchard. Lydia explained that it was important to have multiple shelters so that if danger came, we could go to the nearest one.

Under the kitchen table, a large rug covered a trap door to a small dugout cave-like space where one of us, in a tight squeeze, could crouch for a short amount of time. There was no room for three people in that tiny hideout.

In the barn's hayloft, Jacob had constructed a retreat that was about 3 feet high and about 4 feet wide. Atop this refuge, hay was piled to the ceiling, completely covering it. The patrollers would never have known that was there unless they removed all the hay from the entire hayloft.

Off to one side of the apple orchard, there was an old broken-down red wagon that appeared to be unused and somewhat rotten. It looked like a storage place for the baskets that Jacob used when picking apples. "There are some empty apple baskets inside the wagon. Should you need to hide there, jump up into the wagon and crawl into the corner that is nearly touching the ground. Pull those apple baskets over to hide yourself," Jacob instructed.

Lydia cautioned, "If you are not inside the house when slave catchers come lurking about, either Jacob or I will ring the dinner bell on the front of the house or the back of the barn. Then you must get to the nearest safe spot as quickly as possible."

Jacob told us about a kind of communications system shared by the few abolitionists who lived in the surrounding area. "As soon as the patrollers come near any one of our homes, one of us mounts our fastest horse to gallop at breakneck speed on the shortest route to warn our abolitionist friends.

"With any luck, we will not have to experience any of these scary things," Jacob said, "but we have to be prepared."

The first week passed so quickly and we became so comfortable with the Harlans, it seemed as if we had lived there forever.

Mama was a big help in the house, and I worked in the apple orchards with Jacob. It was getting close to the time that Jacob would be hauling his apples to market and I was excited to be helping him.

Addie's ankle was healing. The swelling had gone down and she was moving about much more easily, still limping, but without pain. Her ankle was no longer black and blue.

She turned out to be perfectly suited to caring for Elise; the whole household warmed with the squeals of laughter coming from both of them.

Ten days after our arrival at the Harlans', a rider appeared to alert Jacob and Lydia that the patrollers were snooping around. He rode off as quickly as he had come.

I was in the orchard with Jacob when Lydia rang the bell. I scampered as quickly as I could into the hideout in the old wagon, following Jacob's instructions.

I waited and waited.

No telling how long I was in the wagon before Jacob came to fetch me. "Come into the house with me, Moses. They've gone now. The women have quite a story to tell," Jacob said.

Mama could hardly get the words out of her mouth quickly enough. She was so excited to tell us what happened.

"When the man told Lydia that the patrollers were snooping around, we moved the kitchen table and the rug. Just in time, we got Addie tucked into that hole."

Lydia picked up the story.

"I put the cover back, then the rug and we moved the table back into position. Before I could figure out what to do with your Mama, there was a loud, relentless banging on the front door. My knees were shaking and knocking. I handed Elise to your Mama and I went to the door," Lydia continued.

"Standing outside the door were two unclean, creepy-looking slave catchers, with hideous scowls on their faces," she said.

"One of them rasped, 'Sorry to bother you, ma'am, but we have orders to retrieve a runaway named Demetry Field and I'm afraid we must search the premises.'"

"I was frightened because your Mama was standing right there," Lydia went on. "I had no idea what they might do about her. I simply nodded and answered, 'I am happy to oblige, sir, but my husband has a rule that I may let no one in the home unless he is present. Right now, he is out in the orchard; you may go find him and bring him back with you. With him present, I will allow you to come in and search our home.'"

"Not even a minute went by and they were back with that same ferocious banging on the front door. I cracked the door slightly, and the two rough ugly men pushed their way into the house using their guns as a threat. Elise started to cry, and your Mama tried to comfort her."

"How did you explain Rebecca's presence?" Jacob asked Lydia.

Lydia explained what happened next.

"One of the slave catchers bellowed at me, 'Who is this nigger?'"

"'Sir, we do not call our slave a nigger,'" I told him. "'This is

Rebecca. She is my house slave. She takes care of our daughter, cleans our home, cooks for us, and sews our clothing,'" I declared.

"You don't need to get so uppity with me, lady," one nasty man said. "Sir, I am not being uppity. Please just do what you need to do and then leave us alone," I told him.

"Quick thinking, my dear. Rebecca, I bet you were terrified; I know I would have been if I were in your shoes," Jacob said.

CHAPTER TWELVE

A Secret Compartment
October 1852

Addie

"I have an idea of how to get you to the next station on the Underground Railroad," Jacob said to the three of us. "In a few days I will need to take the apples to market. I sell them in Cumberland, Maryland and in Uniontown, Pennsylvania. Lydia and I have good friends all along the way, so this is a good opportunity for us to take your family a little farther north on your journey. It will take us one very long day to get to Cumberland, and one day to get to Uniontown."

"Once you are in Pennsylvania, you will be in a free state, though as you know, that does not guarantee your permanent safety. The patrollers and the slave catchers are always sneaking around, looking for a way to reap some reward money.

"I'd like your help loading all of the baskets and getting them into the wagon. We will start today."

"Addie," he spoke directly to me, "are you able to help us?"

"Oh, yes," I replied. I couldn't wait to get out into the orchard to help.

Will we be on the wagon along with the apples? I wondered. I was worried, and could only guess at what might happen if we were seen out on the open road.

Jacob recognized right away what I was thinking. I must have had a frightened expression on my face. "Addie, have I got a surprise for you," he comforted. "Come with me, all of you."

Trudging out to the barn where Jacob kept his wagons, he whispered, "You will now see how creative one must be when helping runaways."

Opening the doors of the barn, we spotted two large wagons. Jacob steered us to the larger wagon that had big red wheels and very high wooden sides. Taking us around to the back of the wagon, Jacob showed us something amazing.

There was a false bottom in the wagon!

We would be stowed away underneath the apples!

Jacob laughed when he saw my mouth hanging open. "You're standing there like you're in some kind of trance. I told you we have to be creative," he said. "One very creative slave named Henry Brown shipped himself in a wooden crate by train from Richmond, Virginia, not too far from where you came from, to Philadelphia. Now that's what I call creative!" Jacob finished.

I was speechless. I had never seen anything quite like that false-bottomed wagon, nor had I heard anything as crazy as mailing yourself in a box! My mind was racing with excitement as I thought about riding in secret underneath Jacob's apple crop.

Jacob cautioned, "Now, Addie, don't be thinking that this will be a joy ride. All three of you are going to be crammed in there tighter than a drum, and the ride will be very uncomfortable. The bottom of the wagon is hard, strong wood covered only with a thin layer of hay to make it a smidgen softer, but I suspect that you will feel every single bump the wagon takes as it moves over the rough trails on our way north. This will not be a jolly undertaking, I assure you." We worked through the day, picking apples and loading them into monster-sized baskets atop the wagon. One more day was needed to finish the task.

Enjoying a delicious and satisfying meal prepared by Lydia and Mama, my thoughts ran all over the place. In another day, we would be moving on again.

The Harlans had become our good friends. We treasured their company and we genuinely felt like a part of their family. I had become so attached to Elise that I could not imagine how I could say good-bye to her.

Mama and Lydia delighted in each other's company in the kitchen. Mama was singing again while she and Lydia teased and joked with one another. Yes, without question, it was going to be painful leaving our new Virginia friends.

We were beginning to understand the feelings of loss - saying goodbye to good friends. Paris, Lafayette, Lizzie, and Rachel. Sarah and James. Missus. Now Lydia, Jacob and Elise. I didn't want to leave their happy household, but, at the same time, I was excited about the next part of our trip. *If we ever reach a place where we can live free, it will all be worth it.*

The morning arrived when we would depart the Winchester apple orchard. Tearfully bidding farewell to Lydia and Elise, we packed ourselves into the bottom of the wagon, Mama and Moses on the outsides and I in the middle with my head at their feet.

Jacob was right. It was miserably tight.

There were minuscule openings around the edges so we would draw fresh air, though at the time I didn't consider that the air would be filled with dust churned up by the wagon wheels as we bounced over the poor roads. I had to grab a corner of my sleeve to place over my mouth to keep from coughing or choking. Mama and Moses did the same.

Mid-morning, we were stopped by three patrollers.

"Sir, whatcha got here on this wagon?" one of the surly men asked Jacob.

"Well, I think you can see," Jacob answered. "I have my crop of Winesap apples to sell at the markets in Cumberland, and in Uniontown, Pennsylvania."

"You hiding any slaves in there, mister?" demanded one of the other two.

We could hear their conversation clearly. The voices of those men were anything but friendly. Terrified, we held our breaths when Jacob answered. "No, I am not. You can look into the wagon and see for yourself. There is no room for anything but apples."

After the three made their inspection of the wagon, we were on our way again. Mama, Moses, and I, stowed away under the weight of the apples, were mighty relieved to be on the move again.

When he was sure that the men were long gone, Jacob stopped so we could get out, have a drink of cool water, chomp on an apple (of course) and make a necessary run into the woods. We jammed ourselves back into our humble hideaway and continued the journey.

Later, we stopped again for a hearty lunch break. But, after that, Jacob only stopped one more time, - late afternoon, I guess. The horses were tired and needed a break and fresh water. Jacob had a funny feeling about something that he couldn't explain, so we scrambled back into our compartment quickly and got back on the trail.

Jacob told me later that we were on the road for more than ten hours that first day, partly because when we arrived at the home of his friend, where we hoped to spend the night, there was something out of order. Something didn't look right.

Jacob expected to see a broom placed upside down on the front porch; instead it was placed right side up, warning that it was not safe to stop there. Heeding the alert, Jacob took us off the path, deep into the nearby woods for what seemed like an eternity. No wonder the ride became so bumpy. I was miserable, being bounced around underneath the heavy load of apples. My head was situated in between Mama's and Moses' feet, so I couldn't see their faces, but I am sure they were as uncomfortable as I was.

Suddenly we took off at a clip when Jacob saw that the broom was changed to the "free from danger" position. We arrived at the home of Jacob's friend in Cumberland just as day turned to night. Jacob introduced us to Joseph and Margaret Ogden. Mrs. Ogden invited us to join them in the dining room for dinner. After a tasty dinner, we were escorted to our sleeping safe haven in their barn. It was an area almost identical to the one in Jacob's hayloft. We climbed in and slept.

In the morning, we were awakened by Jacob as he explained that while he and Moses would be spending the day in the market, Mama and I would help Mrs. Ogden in the field, harvesting potatoes. The fall weather was comfortable and it was a pleasant day to be out in the sunshine after spending such a long day confined to the bottom of the apple cart. We had potatoes in our truck patch, so I knew how to dig potatoes. In fact, I filled those baskets more quickly than both Mama and Mrs. Ogden. We were mighty tired by the end of the afternoon. Mrs. Ogden said, "We better get back to the house. The men will be home soon, and they will be hungry. I need to cook dinner."

"Please, let me help," Mama offered. The three of us worked together preparing a delicious dinner of boiled ham and potatoes. Everyone was tired, so we went to bed early.

Rising early the next morning to get a good start on what promised to be a very long day, we noticed that almost half of the apples had been sold.

My brain was racing. *What if slave catchers can tell that there is a false bottom in the wagon when it is not full of apples?*

I should not have been concerned. Jacob and his friend Joseph had it all figured out way ahead of me. Joseph filled the empty spaces in the wagon with his potatoes and the two friends carried us on our way to Uniontown, Pennsylvania.

Two hours into the ride, Jacob pulled the horse over to a fast-moving stream and opened the back of the wagon so we could get out for a bit.

"Well, here we are," Jacob declared.

"What do you mean, here we are," I stammered. It didn't look to me like we were anywhere.

When he saw my puzzled expression, he announced that we had just crossed the border into Pennsylvania. We were now, for the first time, in a free state.

A free state! I am certain that Jacob and Joseph had never

seen such big smiles. We were so happy. Tears of happiness and gratitude ran down our dusty faces. Moses kept saying, over and over again, "I can't believe it. I can't believe it."

As happy as I was, I couldn't shut out Jacob's words running through my head, "Don't forget, you can still be kidnapped in the North. Those slave catchers will hunt you down, no matter where you are. They are only thinking about the money they will get if they catch you and bring you back. And they can be very mean and violent if they catch you. It's no different than when your Mama was stolen from her family in Africa. Some people just love money more than they like doing the right thing."

Jacob and Joseph described the long distance we still had to travel before arriving in Uniontown so we reloaded ourselves into our temporary shelter and resumed the dangerous and uncomfortable ride.

Just when we thought we were nearing our destination, the apple cart took a colossal tumble. Mama and I bounced over into and slightly atop Moses as the wagon came to an abrupt halt.

"Oh, no," I heard Jacob wail. I was afraid to find out what had happened.

The cart had hit an enormous rut in the road. One wheel had careened down into a ditch; it was broken.

Oh no, is right, I thought. *What if we're caught?*

Helping us out of the wagon, Joseph and Jacob went right to work, bringing the wagon upright. Apples and potatoes were strewn all about. Mama, Moses, and I scurried to return all of them to their baskets. The two strong men succeeded in getting the wagon upright.

Once again, Jacob was prepared. Obviously, he had made this trip many times. Spare wooden spokes stored under the cart came out, and Jacob set about repairing the broken wheel. It took quite some time, but after loading the baskets back onto the cart, and safely stowing us inside, we were travelling along as if nothing had happened.

Reaching the Uniontown farm of the Harlans' friends late in the day was a relief. We were all tired, including the horses. Once again we slept in the barn, but this time, the farmer had constructed a small room behind the hayloft, accessible only through a secret opening behind the hay. You had to know precisely where the door was, so that you didn't have to move too much hay out of the way to find it.

The room was quite pleasant with several bed mats on the floor. There was even a small window through which we could see the full moon. Upon entering, we were shocked and surprised to see two other runaways.

Jacob's friend, Matthew Piggott, introduced us to Elijah and Betsey who had escaped from a cotton plantation in Georgia.

As we sat spellbound by their stories, we realized with gratitude that our trek was far shorter and less dangerous than theirs had been. They had gone for more than five days without any food. Elijah had fought with a slave catcher. After they hit each other a few times, Elijah was successful in thumping the slave

151

catcher on the top of the head with the butt of his gun, stolen from his master. They had endured driving rain storms. Elijah had to shoot and kill a wolf who was about to attack his wife, Betsey. Their saga was undeniably more treacherous than ours and we thought our journey was plenty frightening.

What we came to understand from our new companions was that every single slave who chose to run, faced a daunting and terrifying struggle. Still the dream of freedom far out-weighed the risks. The vision of a brighter day when a slave would be able to work and live as a free person was worth the trials of escape.

Our new friendship with Elijah and Betsey made us more determined than ever to stick with our original plan to make it to Canada where we would be free.

Chapter Thirteen

Mama to the Rescue
November 1852

Moses

After a good night's sleep and a big breakfast, Mr. Piggott asked if Elijah and I would help him with chores in the barn. We were more than happy to help. After all, they were helping us! "Yes, sir," we both answered at the same time. Mrs. Piggott spoke up. "Ladies, I'm sure we'll find something to do."

Once again, Mama shared that she liked to cook and she

would like to help in the kitchen. Betsey admitted that she didn't much like cooking, but she was more than willing to help out with the cleaning. Addie said, "Ma'am, I'll do whatever you'd like me to do," as she got up from her chair and started clearing the dirty dishes from the table.

"No, no rush now, folks," Mr. Piggott said. "Let's sit here a while longer. I am enjoying my coffee and our conversation." After each of us shared a story or two about our experiences of the journey so far, Mr. Piggott finally said, "Okay, let's get to work, men."

Late in the afternoon, Addie came out to the barn to tell us that dinner would be ready soon. "Mrs. Piggott says clean up and come in," she said.

After dinner, Mr. Piggott said, "Rebecca, that was one delicious apple pie!" He looked directly at us and continued, "Now, you have become five. This may make your journey much easier or much more difficult, depending on the circumstances you encounter. I am hopeful that it will be easier as I will conduct you to the river where you can move quickly."

I wondered what he meant about "movin' quickly on the water. I had already had my fill of wading in the river, and we certainly didn't move quickly then with our heavy, wet clothes.

"Gather your things, friends, I am going to show you how you will get to the next station." Mr. Piggott led us outside on a short walk through a stand of apple trees - more apples! He directed us down a slippery bank to the river, where he had a small skiff tied to a tree. "This boat will hold all of you, but there will not be much extra room. Be careful to distribute your weight evenly in the boat. This boat is really meant to hold two comfortably, possibly three grown men."

"Stay close to this side of the river and row as fast as you can. You have good light from the moon right now so you can see where you are going. Avoid the trees hanging over the river because there will be tangled roots under the water that you cannot see.

"As you near the small Pennsylvania town of Washington, you will find an old, white man fishing from the shore. He is a conductor on the railroad. He will take you to the next station in Washington."

Mrs. Piggott put a basket of food into the skiff and we were off. At first, Elijah and I took turns at the oar, but we soon learned that it was much faster with both of us rowing at the same time. Each of us could hold an oar with both hands and stroking through the water evenly, we made rapid progress. It wasn't easy fitting both of us on a seat designed for one person - tight as the teeth in my mouth.

If we slid our butts forward on the seat when we lifted the oars out of the water, and slid back and extended our legs when we put the oars back in the water, and pulled with all of our might, we positively flew along the top of the water. But it was utterly exhausting. Mama and Betsey took their turns so that Elijah and I could get a little rest. Even Addie spent some time at the oars.

I figure that we rowed like that for three or four hours before we simply had to stop. Bringing the skiff to the shore, we tied up to a big silver maple and wearily pulled ourselves out of the boat and laid the oars down on the shore. We walked a few steps, and plopped down at the base of an old maple tree to rest. I might have even dozed. I don't know for sure.

Raring to go again after a welcome breather, Mama, Betsey, and Addie ran off for a necessary run into the deep woods, while Elijah and I headed back to where we had the boat tethered.

Suddenly we heard the *ba da rump, ba da rump* sound of a horse coming nearer and nearer by the second.

The slave catcher hopped off his horse with his gun aimed at us. Letting out a loud snort, he snickered, "This is my lucky day! I got two at a time."

With both of his hands on the gun and extending his arms to their full length, he pointed the gun at our heads. He started walking closer and closer to us. Matching him step for step, we started backing up. We were about to fall right into the river.

I was wondering whether Elijah could swim. I had played in the creek near the plantation, but I was never in water that was over my head. I had no idea how deep the water might be here. I didn't swim well myself. If we ended up in the water, we might be goners.

My knife. I remembered it was in its sheath, strapped around my thigh. I discreetly slid my hand down to the knife handle.

The man caught me moving my hand onto the knife.

"Don't know what you think you can do with that knife, you stupid nigger. I can kill you both with two quick shots."

My knife didn't stand a chance against his gun. My brain was racing, trying to figure out some way out of this disaster. One more step backwards and Elijah and I would be in the river.

Just then, there was a loud *Thwack!* That slave catcher fell to the ground like a brick. He just lay there, dropped in his own tracks.

When I looked up, I saw Mama with a big 'ol grin on her face and an oar in her hand. She'd whacked that bad man so hard on the side of his head that she knocked him out cold.

It took me a second to grasp what had actually happened. Then we couldn't help ourselves; we started laughing.

Elijah cautioned us to get out of there as quickly as we could. We had to do something to keep the slave catcher from coming after us when he came to. Using the rope stored in the skiff, Elijah and I tied the man's hands together and dragged him into the water. We had no intention of letting him drown. We fastened him to the maple tree just high enough so that his head stayed above the water line. Mama removed her head rag and wrapped it around the senseless man's bloody head.

Addie grabbed the slave catcher's gun and handed it to me. I promptly handed it off to Elijah. I didn't want to have a thing to do with any gun. Never having held a gun in my hand, I was certain that the gun would be no help to us if I was the one to use it. I was realistic about it; I could possibly even hurt one of us. Nope, Elijah had to carry the gun.

I knew what to do. I instructed Mama and Betsey to ride the slave catcher's horse, near enough to the water to see us, but not so close that the horse would have uneven footing along the banks. Addie, Elijah and I clambered back into the boat, and we all resumed our voyage.

Moving on the water was easier with less weight in the boat. And, from the looks on their faces, Mama and Betsey were enjoying their ride.

An hour or so passed, and there he was…the old fisherman! We were so glad to see him, and he seemed genuinely glad to see us. He commented that this fishing gimmick was the one way he could help runaways as they navigated the Underground Railroad. "I come here every night just before dawn and pretend that I 'm fishing," beamed the old man.

"Actually some days I do catch some fish, but that is not why I am here. Most days I do not come across any passengers. When I do, I am so happy because I can then help them to find their next station. You have made me a very happy man this morning. Leave the boat here; I will return for it later. Where did you get that horse?"

We explained what had happened.

The kind gentleman had a good laugh. "Now, follow me. We should move as quickly as possible, but, as you can see, at my age, I don't really run anymore. We do need to get you there before it is full daylight."

"Addie, how's that ankle?" I asked.

"Moses, it's just fine."

"OK, then. Mama, you and Betsey - back up on that horse!" The old man took the reins and led us along a winding and well-worn path to a small town where we went through the back yards from house to house until he stopped at a stately, stone mansion right in the middle of town.

He patted me on the back and wished us luck. Taking the horse by the reins, he headed back the way we had come. We never learned his name.

When we knocked on the door, we were greeted warmly and we introduced ourselves to the doctor and his wife who owned the home.

Dr. Edmundson was so soft-spoken and kind that we felt comfortable and at ease almost immediately. His home was as spacious as the Big House. Because it felt so warm and inviting, I thought it was even more beautiful.

Leading the five of us into a large kitchen, he asked each of us our names.

As we took turns introducing ourselves to him, he firmly and graciously shook our hands, a gesture that, until now, we had not experienced. I didn't really ponder it at the time, but, looking back on that handshake now, I recognize that Dr. Edmundson was helping us to feel free, to feel human as opposed to feeling like someone's property.

Dr. Edmundson wanted to know about our journeys. Mama, Addie, and I, started chattering simultaneously. "Wait a minute, wait a minute," the doctor smiled as he quieted us. "One at a time, please. I'm not such a good listener that I can hear three stories at once!"

We took turns telling our stories. When we finished, Dr. Edmundson told us that he was proud of us for having endured so much to get to the free state of Pennsylvania. No white man had ever told me that he was proud of me. My heart filled up. My spirits lifted. I wanted that moment to last forever.

Two women working in the large kitchen prepared an enormous breakfast feast for us to enjoy, sitting together like family, at the giant dining table. The doctor and his wife sat with us and asked us to join hands while he prayed silently for a few moments after which he spoke, "God, my family is thankful that these passengers have found their way to our home. Grant them peace. Amen."

Mrs. Edmundson took us upstairs to show us where we would sleep during our time in their home. Elijah and Betsey were led to a comfortable bedroom, Mama and Addie to another, and I to a third. Each room had handsome beds with fine bed-coverings. I wondered what it would feel like to sleep in a room by myself. *Would I feel alone? Or, would I feel like I was my own master?*

Though she surely must have noticed our eyes wide with awe at such lovely surroundings, she said nothing.

Then she showed us something that really did surprise us.

Bathrooms with running water! I had never seen a bathroom where you could stand in a tub and have water run over you. It was called a "shower". There was a seat with a lid. Mrs. Edmundson told us it was a "toilet". You sat on a wooden seat. When you finished, you pulled a cord and everything went away. She explained that water was pumped from the first-floor laundry room, where it was heated, up to the cisterns in the attic. She had to spend quite some time teaching us how to use these unfamiliar things. I was completely astonished. The homes we had visited before coming to the Edmundson's had bathrooms for washing, but no running water. They all used outdoor privies, just as we had at The Porter Plantation.

Mrs. Edmundson invited us to accompany her to a massive room at the back of the house, filled with clothing. We thought we had seen a lot of clothes at the Harlan's, but their collection of donated clothing was small compared to what we saw at the Edmundson's. There was rack after rack of dresses, pants, jackets, and shirts. Shelves on two walls were filled with hats, shoes, stockings, underwear, and shawls.

"Friends, please make yourselves at home here and select whatever items you think you may need. We want you to have at least three full changes of clothing, including underwear, socks and shoes. And you will want to choose a warm jacket or coat; our fall weather is getting quite cold in the evenings. So, go to it now, and take exactly what you like."

Four days at the Edmundson's found us completely rested,

clean, and well-fed. During that time, the doctor told us about his five married adult children who themselves owned properties along the route of the Underground Railroad, and who would help us on our journey to Canada.

Late one morning, Mrs. Edmundson gathered us all together in the grand entry foyer. "In a few moments, Jonathan, a gentleman who works with us, will bring the stagecoach around to the front of the house. He will take you on the next leg of your escape to freedom. You will be quite comfortable, and we have prepared food and drink for your trip. I have written a pass that explains that Jonathan is taking you to a new slave owner. Of course, that's not true, but you have to have an excuse to be on the road. This part of the Underground Railroad is not patrolled as tightly as the routes in eastern Pennsylvania, where most slaves run to get to New York City. You have chosen a good route, one that is less traveled. I don't think you'll need the pass. But one cannot be too careful. The seven-hour ride will take you to the home of our oldest son Ralph. He and his wife, Anna, live in a small town on Chartiers Creek, Bridgeville, a spot near the fork of the Beaver and Mahoning Rivers. Many people stop there to trade and sell goods to one another," she continued.

"There is a gentleman in Bridgeville, Mr. Anthony Cooper, a very good friend of ours, who operates a small printing office. Like us, he is a Quaker who silently plays his part in helping slaves. He will prepare papers declaring that you are free," Mrs. Edmundson said.

But I know that we aren't free. I don't understand.

"As you know, Pennsylvania is a free state, but with the passage of the Slave Act of 1850, you are still at risk of being arrested and driven back to your Master," she continued. "The law calls you 'fugitives,' and it requires that we assist in the capture of runaway slaves. Any person aiding a runaway is to be fined $500 and a six-month prison sentence. So, you can see," she said, "it is critical that you are seen as 'free.'"

As day turned to dusk, the stagecoach entered a small village of perhaps twenty or thirty cottages, one of which became our home for the night.

Ralph Edmundson and his wife Anna were cordial and sociable hosts; the conversation at the dinner table was lively and open. We were slowly getting used to eating at the same table with white people.

We were also learning about entering into discussion and chatting as if our opinions really mattered. Papa and Paris always told me that I mattered and they let me tell them what I thought, but it was hard to be convinced when Ben and Massa made me feel that I wasn't worth anything.

Anna asked Addie several questions about life at the Porter Plantation. She asked in such a way that we sensed that she truly was curious, but not in a way that made us think she was just being nosy.

Addie had certainly found her tongue after we left Culpeper. She went on and on about her sewing, about Missus teaching us to read and write, about abusive Massa, and about our friends, James and Sarah. It made Mama happy to hear Addie carrying on so; she was smiling from ear-to-ear.

Next it was my turn. Ralph asked me to tell him how I had learned about abolitionists and how I had learned what I needed to know to become a runaway. Once I got going, I simply couldn't stop talking. Flying out of my mouth were the stories of my time with Paris and of the lessons learned from Papa. Suddenly, I could not continue. I tried hard not to cry, but a few tears ran down my cheeks, as I wished Papa were with us on this journey.

I figure Mama was starting to feel at home with the Edmundsons too, because all of a sudden, she started blurting out the story of how she was kidnapped from her family in Africa and led in chains for days to the boat that would carry her across the ocean to be sold as a slave in Virginia. Mama repeated the story she had told us many days ago, when we began our journey. This time, though, she was quiet and calm as she related her saga to the Edmundsons. We were crammed in the hold with hundreds of others. We had very little food and what we had tasted terrible. I don't even know what you would call that mush. They gave us almost no water. We stayed down in that cargo hold where there was no daylight." Mama paused, "Many died."

As Mama talked, I wondered how many of our friends in the slave quarters had come across the ocean in that way. And I wondered why Paris, or Mama, or Papa had not told us this part of our history; perhaps some things were just too difficult to remember and to talk about. I made a decision right then and there, that if I ever reached freedom, I would tell Mama's story. I could be her voice. I could be the voice of many. Everyone needs their voices to be heard.

CHAPTER FOURTEEN

Forgery
November 1852

Addie

Early in the evening, just after dinner, there was a knock on the door. I was suddenly terrified: we'd just heard the doctor's wife explain about the law that might take us from a free state back to a slave state like Virginia.

Was someone coming to arrest us and take us back to Virginia? Were they going to arrest Ralph and Anna?

Ralph noticed the worried look on my face, and he caught me picking at the skin around my fingernails. He took my two hands in his and said, "Addie, there is nothing to worry about. This will be our friend, Anthony Cooper, who will prepare your freedom documents. Don't be surprised when you receive your papers. We will have to change your name so that your slave-holders can't track you down."

Mr. Cooper led me back into the dining room where the table had been cleared. He had papers laid out in five separate piles. Taking the first stack of paper, he began to ask me questions. His manner was calm and quiet. I was no longer afraid.

"Addie, I'm going to ask you many questions. Don't be scared. I'm here to help you," Mr. Cooper began. What is the name of the plantation where you lived? Do you know where it is located? What is the Master's full name? How long were you enslaved on the Porter Plantation? What were your duties? How many slaves worked on the plantation? Where did you live - in the slave quarters or in the master's house? Were you a quiet slave or a sassy one?" On and on it went, until Mr. Cooper was finally finished asking questions and writing down my answers on the forms in front of him.

Next Mr. Cooper measured me to see how tall I was. He noted the color of my eyes, skin, and hair. He looked carefully to see if I had any noticeable scars.

When he was finished, we walked to the parlor where the others waited their turns. I gave everyone a big smile, so they would know that it was okay. One by one, we went through the process of giving Mr. Cooper the information he needed to create our forged free documents. When he finished, he and Mr. Edmundson chatted quietly for a short time. As he left, he smiled at all of us, "You will have your free papers tomorrow morning."

We understood that we would not yet truly be free, but to have a piece of paper that said we were free seemed good enough.

At breakfast the next morning, we were each handed our papers. I studied mine carefully. It was a formal, legal-looking document with a fancy scroll border. Inside the border in the upper left-hand were the words *State of Virginia, County of Culpeper.* There was a number in the right-hand corner, 3216. I had no idea if the number meant anything at all.

The words on the page said: Adeline Connell, a free woman of color, who was heretofore registered in the Clerk's Office of the Court in Culpeper, Virginia is granted renewal of her freedom papers originally signed 11 October 1851. Then followed a full description of my size, age, complexion, and job title, seamstress. There appeared to be a signature of Massa and one of Mr. Cooper. It was dated October 11, 1852.

I knew that it wasn't real, but it looked mighty good to me. Each of us settled into our own thoughts as we studied our new papers.

We still had days to go before we would reach Canada, but I could not help but feel extremely grateful for the generosity and kindness shown to us by so many along the way.

Gathering our small leather satchels filled with our new clothes, we thanked Anna and joined Ralph in the horse-drawn carriage waiting for us at the front door.

"Your papers will be important in this next part of your journey to Canada. In about an hour we will arrive at the train station in Pittsburgh. From there you will travel for about two hours and will get off the train at Brighton. As soon as you get off the train, find a porter and ask where you should go to catch the northwest line to Ashtabula, Ohio," Ralph instructed.

"Now you will be on the real railroad," he added. "Your tickets have been purchased for you by the abolitionist society. There is a ticket for the portion of the trip from Pittsburgh to Brighton, and another for the final leg to Ashtabula. Don't lose them. Keep your papers with you at all times."

I was nervous and jumpy, but, at the same time, I was excited and keyed up about riding in a train on real train tracks. I heard that there was a railroad being built between Charlottesville and Richmond, but I didn't really understand what a railroad was.

Ralph's remark about the 'real' railroad was pretty funny, because we had been talking about riding on the Underground Railroad ever since we left Front Royal, and it was never a railroad and it was not underground.

Ralph continued, "A conductor will pass through the cars just after the train leaves the station. He will ask to see your ticket and he will also ask to see your papers. Act as if you have been doing this all your life. Do not show any fear, or he will get suspicious. Once he is satisfied that you are a legitimate passenger, he will punch your ticket and you will ride freely to Brighton."

"Mr. Ralph," I asked, "You said to ask a porter for directions to the northwest line once we get off the train in Brighton. What's a porter?"

"Good question, Adeline. A porter is a person who helps passengers with the luggage and answers questions. You can tell a porter by his cap and his jacket. He wears a small cap with a squared crown and a small bill. His jacket is short, and ends at his waist."

We stood on the railway platform, waiting for the time when we could board the train. There was so much noise and commotion. Workers were everywhere. One man was pounding on the wheels of the railcar right next to me. He was using a large hammer-like thing that I had never seen before. The repetitive sound it made was ear-piercing; I had to cover my ears. I didn't think he would ever stop. I had no idea what he was doing, but I wondered if it had something to do with whether or not the wheel was attached properly. I sure hoped it was. Some soot-covered men threw shovelful after shovelful of coal into the firebox, laughing and joking with each other as they worked. I smiled when I noticed how white their teeth seemed against their sooty faces.

The engineer must have been testing the whistle; the

steam engine hissed loudly. Stewards were scurrying along the platform carrying huge trays of food to the dining car. By the time the conductor finally gave us permission to board, I was overwhelmed by all that was going on around me. I found it hard to concentrate on the steps when I climbed up onto the train, and I stumbled. Embarrassed, I started to gather up my things. A nice man helped me and put my bag in a rack above my seat. "I'm a porter, ma'am. I'm glad to help," he said. Ah, so that's a porter!

"Tickets, tickets," called the conductor as he entered our car.

Oh, oh, I thought. *Here goes.*

I hope I can act like this is an everyday experience for me.

Don't fumble.

Smile.

Look natural.

He was a tall, black man who reminded me of Papa, tall and skinny, with a soft kind look on his face. I handed him my ticket. He looked me over carefully, then asked to see my papers. I wondered what he was thinking as he looked them over. Giving me a short nod, he moved on to the others. I tried to relax and enjoy my first train ride.

We arrived in Brighton on schedule. Getting off the train, my eyes darted around, looking for a porter. Spotting one not too far from me, I confidently headed toward him and asked, "Pardon me, sir, but will you show me where to catch the northwest line to Ashtabula, Ohio?"

"Sure, Miss, follow me," he said. I motioned to the others to follow.

"That train should arrive here in thirty minutes. You will board over there on Platform 3. Walk ahead to the front of this train, and then you can cross over to the right platform. Look for the signs above your heads. You will see the sign for number 3. I will be there in time to help you board the correct train," he said, as he stepped away from me to help others with their bags.

The conductor on the second train was not nearly as nice as the first one. As he entered our car and bellowed, "Tickets, tickets," he scowled and looked at us as if we had no right to be on the train. His big belly hung over his pants and he couldn't button the last two buttons on his jacket. My first impression of him made me feel like my old sassy self. I really wanted to punch him in that fat stomach. Just in time, I remembered how I had to get along when the Massa was around.

Lower my head slightly.

Put that phony smile on my face.

It works every time.

That conductor studied my papers for what seemed like forever. "You sure you're not some runaway nigger?" he sneered with his lower jaw jutted out as if he were about to bite me.

"Oh no, sir," I answered, "why would you ask that?"

"Runaways like to get to Ashtabula," he said.

That's all he said to me, but he gave Moses and Elijah a tough time before he finally moved on to the other passengers.

Three hours later, we arrived in Ashtabula, met by Dr. Edmundson's daughter Elizabeth, wearing a warm smile and a bright red wool cape.

I was so happy to survive, not one train ride, but two! I was still a little afraid, but I was actually starting to look at our journey as an adventure. *What will we do here in Ashtabula? Why are we here? Where are we going anyway? Will I be as afraid as I was that first night when we stood in the water all night?*

Chapter Fifteen

Rough Waters
November 1852

Moses

The sun was just beginning to peek out at us as we arrived at Lake Erie that crisp October morning. Dr. Edmundson's daughter Elizabeth delivered us to the steamboat in Ashtabula, that would take us across the lake to Buffalo.

Elijah and Betsey were wearing grins from one side of their faces to the other. Mama was singing away like there was no tomorrow. It was like she had to sing every song she ever knew.

Addie was fidgety and jumpy, moving like a crazy little bird poking its beak into the ground from one place to another until it finds a worm. One moment she primped, checking her clothes to be sure that she looked fine. Then, suddenly she was hopping about here and there laughing. A minute later, she plopped down on the ground and started sobbing. Mama sat beside her and calmed her down, just as Addie had quieted Mama when she told us the story of her capture in Africa.

It was no surprise to anyone that I was the quiet one. Though not obvious to anyone else, my stomach was doing somersaults while I kept rubbing that stone in my pocket, flipping it over and over again, tapping the pointed end with my finger.

I had only heard about the ocean, the ocean that carried Mama from Africa to the shores of Virginia many years ago. As I stared out at the enormous body of water in front of us, I felt sure that the ocean could not possibly be any larger than Lake Erie. There was water as far as I could see. I couldn't see a shore out there anywhere...just the one I was standing on. Now of course I know better, but the sheer size of the water that would carry us to Canada was overwhelming...my brain just couldn't absorb it.

There was a lot of activity buzzing about the wooden steamboat. Workmen were attending to every detail before the boat could set off on its way.

Great amounts of wood were necessary to power the boiler of the steam engine. It seemed like it took forever to stack and take all of it down to the main deck where the steam engine was located. Crates of wheat, corn, apples, and pears were also taken to the cargo hold.

The upper deck was built to accommodate passengers. There were many of us waiting on the dock until it would be our turn to get onto the steamship. Standing with Elijah and Betsey, we found ourselves paying careful attention to all of the other passengers. Some travelers were dressed in very fancy clothes and it appeared that they were going off on some sort of adventure.

Somewhat surprising to us was the fact that also gathered together on the platform were many other black families with some white folks who appeared to be their sponsors, just like Elizabeth was for us.

My curiosity was getting the best of me. I was crazy to strike up a conversation and to learn more about them, but I did my best to keep that in check until a more appropriate time. I contented myself by keeping my eyes and ears open, like Papa always said. We knew that we would be aboard the ship for about five days. There would be plenty of time to get to know our fellow passengers.

By the time we left Ashtabula, Ohio, we had enjoyed the compan-
ionship and warm hospitality of three of Dr. Edmundson's grown
children. We were treated grandly by all of them. The hospitality
shown to us by the entire family was slightly overwhelming and
it started me thinking.

Paris had always told me that I thought about things way
more than the average person. Perhaps he was right. He never
suggested that I was wrong to dwell on things so much, just that
I seemed to put myself into another place thinking.

And thinking and thinking.

Before we left the plantation, I could not get the idea of
slavery out of my mind. It popped up constantly; I could not
figure out how somebody could buy another person and then
put them to work and control every aspect of their lives. How
could Massa do that to all of us? What right did he have? I knew
we had to get away from slavery if we possibly could.

Meeting Dr. Edmundson's family started me thinking about
something else: we could not have accomplished our escape
from slavery without the help of others. We could not have done
it on our own.

Period.

Running over and over in my head were the many people
helped us along The Underground Railroad: Paris, Missus,
James and Sarah, Lydia and Jacob, the bonesetter, Jacob's friends,

the old fisherman, Mr. and Mrs. Piggott, the entire Edmundson family, Anthony, the printer who made our new identification papers, the friendly porter, the carriage driver....

The thing was, I didn't know what to do about my thoughts. I knew what I had to do when I was thinking about slavery all the time back at the plantation. I had to run away. I had to escape it. But I didn't know what to do about these new thoughts occupying my brain. It took me a long time to understand the symbol of my freedom stone. I would figure out what I should do about these thoughts, too.

While I was lost in thought, Elizabeth stepped up to me and handed me three tickets. She handed tickets to Elijah and Betsey.

"When you reach the far eastern tip of Lake Erie, you will be in Buffalo, New York, not Canada. Look for a tall man who will be wearing a top-hat. He will hold a sign that says 'Moses.' My father sent him your name by telegram, Moses, back when you were staying with my parents in Washington. That man is my father's friend, Peter. Now, I don't want to frighten you, but you will need to be careful. There are often slave catchers hanging around on the docks, hoping to catch runaways. As soon as you spot Peter, run to him and greet him with these words: 'Elizabeth sends you her love.' His carriage will be waiting. He will whisk you - quick as a wink - across the border into Canada."

She gave all of us a hug, kissed Mama, Addie, and Betsey on the cheek, and shook Elijah's and my hands. With a quick wave, she was off.

We were pushed and shoved along the gangplank as everyone was eager to get aboard the steamship. I worried about Addie and Mama. I didn't want to lose them in the crowd; we held hands once again, carrying our satchels in our free hands. We had to bear the sneers of those who thought that our way of sticking together slowed them down, but I didn't care. We had come too far on our journey to lose sight of each other now.

Once aboard, we were directed to an area where we gathered to hear instructions from the crew. All of the black people on the ship were assigned to one crew leader. I don't know where the white people were gathered. I know that some were fancy passengers, so I guess they probably had their own special group somewhere atop the ship.

"Listen to me, now," the big and burly black man hollered over the noise of the steam engine. "We have made many trips from Ashtabula to Buffalo, but they are not always easy, especially at this time of year. When the air is as cold as it is today and the water is still warm, we could have snow along with blustery, strong winds.

"Lake Erie is also known for its violent thunderstorms. If we have a thunderstorm during our voyage, I guarantee that you will never - for as long as you live - forget the lightning. It is as beautiful as it is frightening. Just three months ago, there was a terrible shipwreck of the paddlewheel steamer, the PSS Atlantic.

It was rammed by a propeller steamer and the Atlantic sank just off of Long Point. We are taking the long route to Buffalo because the people directly across the lake would not welcome you as kindly as the Canadians in Niagara Falls. The waters going due north from here are more unfriendly as well. The journey is longer this way, but far safer. I do not want to worry you unnecessarily, but you must be aware of the risks you undertake as we begin our crossing from here to Buffalo.

"If a storm comes up, move quickly to the inside walls of the boat and wrap your arms tightly around one of the many vertical support posts all around the deck. Several of you will need to be clinging to the same post. Grab onto anything sturdy and solid, and hang on for dear life.

"Enough, now. There are plenty of chairs and benches on the deck for you to watch the other boats on the lake when the weather is good. Be cautious, but not afraid. Try to enjoy the passage to Buffalo," he finished as he turned and walked away.

Elizabeth didn't tell us about this. After we have come this far, now I have to worry that our boat might sink in a bad thunderstorm?

I did everything I could to appear confident and unafraid, even while my knees were banging against each other. I could almost hear Missus reminding me, *"Bravery is doing what you have to do, even when you are terribly afraid. And, I know you are brave, Moses."*

Luckily, there was only one heavy rainstorm that created four

181

foot swells during our passage. The boat rocked and bounced about for several hours. We hung on to sturdy pillars or door jambs. Some people got sick. I heard someone call that "being seasick". But there was no lightning or thunder. The boat did not sink.

The sun was shining brightly on a chilly morning when the steamboat finally docked in Buffalo. All of the passengers on board were gathered, pushing and shoving along the rails to get a glimpse of the boatmen taking cargo and baggage off the boat.

People were cheering and laughing. Some, including Mama and Addie, were crying. I was nervous. *Would I recognize Peter? Would he recognize us? What if he wasn't there? If he wasn't there, we would be right where the slave catchers could capture us. If he is there, how long would it take to get from Buffalo to the border? Will we be safe along the way?*

As the gangway was put into place, my eyes scanned the waiting crowd for a top-hat. "Ah, Mama, there he is! There, over there," I said, pointing to where he stood.

The passengers were in a rush to get off the steamship. I was excited to get off too, but I was still scared about what might happen next. Finally, it was our turn to leave the boat. We walked carefully down the shaky gangplank, each carrying our own bag. As soon as my feet hit the ground, I grabbed Mama's hand, she grabbed Addie's, and we ran toward Peter. Elijah and Betsey followed. We must have been a sight…attached by the hands with our suitcases bumping against our legs as we ran.

When we got close to the man with the top-hat, I finally saw the sign with my name on it. I breathed a sigh of relief. Showing more confidence than I really felt, I walked straight up to him and said, "Elizabeth sends you her love." He smiled. "Now, quickly, come with me," he said. We followed him to his carriage - a very large covered carriage with curtains over the windows, and pulled by four horses. The driver hopped down from his perch atop the carriage, lifted our bags into the back, and helped us inside.

Once we were all inside, Peter asked, "Do you all have your papers handy?"

"Oh no," I thought Now what? *Are we going to be stopped?*

Peter told us that the ride to the border would take just one hour with the horses galloping at full speed. He explained that there was a possibility that we might be stopped by patrollers, but he added that it had never happened when he was in charge and he did not expect it to happen to us. "You must be prepared, just in case." I had heard that before!

The road was better than the gravel or mud roads we were used to. It was quite smooth. I was grateful for that because the horses seemed to be flying, and we were getting jostled about. Mama and Betsey napped some. Elijah and I talked nervously about all of the things that worried us. Addie fidgeted.

I began to relax as the horses picked up speed. Peter noticed that I seemed calmer than I had been earlier. "Moses, the trip is less scary from here on. The patrollers don't bother coming this far. They are too lazy. They would rather catch runaways right at the docks than spend so much time along these roads," Peter said.

All of a sudden, the horses slowed, and finally stopped. I pulled the curtain back and peeked out. I didn't see anything other than a small creek nearby.

"Don't worry now, friends. We have to stop for a little bit, so the horses can rest, have some oats, and some water. You should get out for a while yourselves. We will share some food over there under that big tree near the creek," Peter said, pointing to the tree.

Maybe we will make it after all.

When we were all out of the carriage, Peter said with a huge grin on his face, "We have just crossed the border. You are now in Canada."

Did I hear him correctly? Are we really in Canada? Papa, I wish you were with us too.

We made it! We made it!

We were free!

Mama broke out into song. Singing more loudly than I had ever heard, she began. One by one, we joined her, until we were one, very loud, very happy chorus.

Free at last, free at last,
Thank God I'm free at last.
Free at last, free at last,
Thank God I'm free at last.

CHAPTER SIXTEEN

Letters from old friends
1865-1867

June 15, 1865

Mr. James Porter
The Porter Plantation
Culpeper, Virginia

My friend James,

I am unsure of the mailing address I should use, so it is my hope that this letter reaches you. During the last thirteen years, I have wanted to talk with you many times. Now that the war is over, I'd like to renew our friendship.

Mama, Addie, and I arrived in Canada in November 1852. Some Canadians were angry about the arrival of so many escaped slaves, because they feared that it would be difficult, if not impossible, to settle so many into their country. They also charged, wrongly, in my opinion, that slaves would be likely to commit violent crimes. Many slaves arrived on the same day, and on the same steamship that brought us. There were so many steamships carrying escaped slaves on Lake Erie then, it was like a traffic jam on the water.

Other Canadians acted all high and mighty, as if they were superior to the American slaveholders, because they themselves would never have owned slaves. Canada was a British colony, and Britain had abolished slavery in 1833.

Horace Gerald, who met us at the ship, was like neither of these. He was a good man who was willing to do whatever it took to help us get started in our new community. Mr. Gerald was a part-owner of a large hotel in Niagara Falls. He hired me as a porter in The Carteret Hotel. He, his wife, and their two children, lived in a mansion a few blocks from the hotel. They hired Mama as their personal cook and set us up in a small apartment above the building where their carriages were stored. Addie helped Mama when she was not in school. Mr. and Mrs. Gerald were kind and helpful. They found a good school that would accept us, which was not an easy prospect at the time.

Addie and I loved going to school. To be allowed to learn was such a new concept for us, we could hardly believe our good fortune. After secondary school, Addie got a job as a seamstress in a grand hotel in Niagara and it was there that she met her husband.

I continued working full-time at the hotel, while studying part-time at university. I knew I wanted to become a teacher. Starting from the moment that you and your mother began teaching us to read and write, learning became an important focus of my life. My wife Hannah and I met at university and were married in 1861. I completed my degree last year, and we both are first-year teachers in a colored school in New York City.

188

I am eager to learn about you and your family. We have worried and wondered what happened to you, your dear mother and sister, when you returned home without us that September in 1852. I look forward to hearing from you.

Sincerely,

Moses Porter
330 West 30th Street
Apartment 687
New York, New York

August 11, 1865

Mr. Moses Porter
330 West 30th Street
Apartment 687
New York, New York

Dear Moses,

What a great surprise to hear from you! The address you used got to me just fine, because the people in the post office in Culpeper know me and routed the letter directly to my post office box. You might add the box number, 135, to your next letter, but it is not absolutely necessary.

Father died in February, 1860, when I was 24. He was so worked up about the idea that there could be a war and that he might lose his slaves that, for the last two years of his life, he yelled and screamed all the time at anyone and everyone. He continued to drink too much. You have heard the expression, "he dug his own grave". I think that definitely applied to Father. He died of a heart attack.

Mother took over the plantation, which she managed more kindly than did Father. She discovered that she was a skilled businesswoman while I was away at the University of Virginia, studying the law.

Mother offered the slaves their freedom, though she worried

190

that if they all left, she would have no field hands to work the tobacco fields. No one chose to leave, but they all appreciated having papers that declared them free. Mother worked hard to gain their trust and to pay them when she could after the sale of the tobacco. Meanwhile, she utilized the talents of her former slaves to create other small businesses in which they all shared: blacksmithing, sewing, cooking, and furniture making. I must tell you that Cuffy makes beautiful furniture. He has made and sold elegant roll-top desks, tables with graceful curved legs, and handsome wood beds. Mother's most innovative venture was to start planting peach trees. Slowly but surely she moved away from the tobacco business and maintained a smaller, but steadier income. She sold 200 acres to Frederick Adams, and she gave five acres to each family living on the property.

My wife and I married at Christmastime in 1860, barely ten months after Father passed away. We were still newlyweds when the war broke out. We have two children, a daughter and a son.

We both wish you and your family a Happy Thanksgiving. Surely we have a lot to be thankful for, not the least of which is our good friendship.

Fondly,
James

January 29, 1866

Mr. James Porter
The Porter Plantation
Post Office Box 135
Culpeper, Virginia

Dear James,

Happy New Year! We enjoyed having our family together during the Christmas holidays. Addie and her husband Robert live in Niagara Falls with their children, ages 4 and 2. All of them, including Mama, arrived by train on December 23rd. We were tightly crammed into our small apartment, but we had a wonderful time together decorating the tree and baking Christmas star cookies.

Mama still lives in Niagara Falls, in the same apartment where she has lived since our arrival in 1852. She doesn't work much anymore, but the family who owns the apartment is so fond of her that they don't want her to leave.

To pick up where I left off in my last letter...I had not finished my degree when the war started in the United States. Shortly after it began, I joined a Negro Regiment on the side of the North. Everything about it felt strange to me. I had been raised in the South, but the North represented the anti-slavery movement. I worried about you, because I assumed that you were fighting the same war, but on the side of the South. I remembered the story Paris had told me about Nat Turner, and I wondered if I could I really kill someone. I didn't think I could. Fortunately, I never had to. I worked as a medic in a mobile hospital. I did my best; I know that I saved some lives, but I was not adequately trained for the job.

It also seemed odd that, the Union Army, fighting to end slavery, treated Black Union soldiers differently than white soldiers. We received lower pay and then had to pay for our clothing out of our pay. The white soldiers received higher pay and did not have to pay for their clothes. Some white officers had low opinions of us. They didn't believe we were as smart as white soldiers, so they didn't spend as much time training us.

I was mighty glad when the war was over and I hoped that we could all return to some sort of a normal life. Who knows what is 'normal' anymore? If the way we are living today is normal, I know we have a lot of work to do. I pray that when my students are as old as I am today, they will not face the discrimination that I still face. Perhaps it was too much to hope that it would end with the Emancipation Proclamation.

I am still waiting to hear if you were punished when Massa noticed that we were missing. Stay in touch. I enjoy hearing from you.

Fondly,
Moses

March 14, 1866

Mr. Moses Porter
330 West 30th Street
Apartment 687
New York, New York

Dear Moses,
When the war broke out, we were living with Mother on the plantation. We all had very mixed feelings about the war. It was frightening to think that some of our friends would be fighting and dying for a cause that we did not believe in. Even though we were abolitionists at heart, we did not want our neighbors to lose their livelihood if and when they had to set their slaves free.

For many reasons, most of which must be obvious to you, Moses, I just couldn't fight. Though I am not proud of it, when I was drafted, I used our wealth to purchase a position for myself as a journalist reporting on the war. It was dangerous enough, but I was not carrying a weapon.

After the war, since our slaves had already been freed, there was not an upheaval at our home as there was at many others. It was a sad time for the South, but a hopeful time for the country. Of course, we were able not only to understand but also feel the sadness and the hope. My family worked with many others to begin the important work of reconstruction in Culpeper. The town was a crossroad for both the Northern and Southern armies, and it had been badly damaged.

Oh, yes. I keep forgetting. You want to know what happened after we left you that September. After a nice visit in Front Royal, we headed back to Culpeper, worried about what Father would say when he found out that you were gone. All the way home, we tried out all kinds of different stories that we might tell him. None of them sounded very realistic, so we finally decided that we would simply say that we had no idea when you might have run away, since we weren't at home. He would not have known that you were with us. We knew that he would be angry, but we figured that he would assume that the slaves were under the eyes of Ben, the overseer, and we might escape punishment entirely.

Father arrived home from Richmond before we returned from Front Royal. Was he in a stew! Nobody knows why, but for some reason, Ben had run off.

In Ben's absence four more slaves, Israel, Exeter, Hanson, and Flemming, had escaped. Father was short seven slaves. He raged for days about how stupid Ben was and about how he couldn't believe that he had hired such a dunce. We were spared! He never once considered that we might have played any role in your absence.

The slave catchers were called in, but, because they were so late in starting the search, not one slave was ever found. Mother, Sarah, and I secretly enjoyed Father's ranting, but of course we acted as if it had been a truly terrible thing.

Somehow, Mother convinced Father to hire Lafayette, as the new overseer. I have no idea how she accomplished this; I am guessing she convinced him on an evening when he was either very tired or had enjoyed too much Virginia lightning. Lafayette was trusted by all the former slaves. There was no more whipping or hollering. Not surprisingly, the workers were much more productive, working harder and faster. They harvested as much tobacco as they had earlier, but this time with fewer people. Amazing. If Father hadn't been so anxious about the pending war, he might have noticed how smoothly Lafayette ran the tobacco production.

I've rambled way too long, dear friend. I look forward to hearing from you soon.

Fondly,
James

April 15, 1866

Mr. James Porter
The Porter Plantation
Post Office Box 135
Culpeper, Virginia

Dear James,

It is good that you and your family helped in the reconstruction of Culpeper. There was so much damage from the war - on both sides. It will be many years before our country heals itself after this devastation. If I had been there, I would have helped too.

We have so many shared memories. My friends are always amazed when I tell them about the good times on the Porter Plantation. Most people can't understand that there could possibly be anything remotely pleasant about living in slavery. There were many very difficult and sad times. Of course, I did not like being a slave. But, didn't we have some good times? I'll never forget the stinking dead fish we put in Massa's study. And I remember how much fun we had up in our hideout in the hayloft. Nobody had to know what we were doing up there. It was our secret place. I still appreciate how much time you spent teaching me to read.

I have another question, James. I have wondered about it for a long time. How is it that your Mother knew about the little white farmhouse where the Harlans greeted us so warmly?

197

Soon we will complete the school year. Hannah and I look forward to summer break. However, summer is not truly a vacation for us. Most of the boys and girls in our school are left alone during the day as their parents or grandparents work. Our concern is that over the summer, these children will lose some of what they learned during the school year so we have set up classes, field trips, and art and music lessons for the months of July and August. Some of the local businesses have agreed to help us financially and others will provide the necessary supplies, lunches, and snacks. It is quite the organizational feat, but we hope it will be worthwhile.

I look forward to hearing from you again soon. Tell me about your law practice.

Fondly,
Moses

July 18, 1866

Mr. Moses Porter
330 West 30th Street
Apartment 687
New York, New York

Dear Moses,

Of course, you have wondered about how Mother knew the Harlans. You will remember that we were going to visit Mother's sister Aunt Abigail in Front Royal when Mother decided to send you on your way to the Harlans.

Aunt Abigail and her husband are abolitionists. They had long been active conductors on the Underground Railroad themselves. I am sure that Mother talked with them often about this whenever she had the occasion to visit them as she was adamantly opposed to slavery even though we ourselves owned slaves. A difficult position for Mother indeed. So, it is my best guess that she learned about the various routes on the Underground Railroad from Abigail.

My aunt's family was well-known to the patrollers. Slaves were regularly being captured near their home in Front Royal. I think this is the reason that Mother chose a safer route for you.

I have recently read a book that I think you would find interesting. I am sending it to you separately. Let me know what you think of it after you have had time to read it. The book is a novel written by William Wells Brown called *The President's Daughter*. It is a fictional account of two slave sisters who were daughters of President Thomas Jefferson. The author himself escaped from slavery in 1834. The book was published in London where he moved to avoid re-capture after the Fugitive Slave Act of 1850. The book describes the effects of slavery on those formerly enslaved. You and I can have some good discussions about it.

Stay in touch, dear friend.

Fondly,
James

April 20, 1867

Mr. Moses Porter
330 West 30th Street
Apartment 687
New York, New York

Dear Moses,

I don't know how to break this news gently. Mother has died. She has been ill for quite some time. The doctors have told us that she had cancer for a long time before she admitted to us that she was feeling unwell, so it was not possible to save her.

The sadness I feel knows no bounds. Mother was a fine woman and a good friend. Sarah and I were so fortunate to have her guide us as we grew up in an angry household. She always found ways to bring joy into our lives. Her smile will never be forgotten.

I know how much Mother meant to you as well. I am so sorry to share this painful news.

Mother's funeral will be on April 25 at Mitchell's Presbyterian Church with graveside services at Fairview Cemetery. I am sure that it would be a great difficulty for you to come, but if you are able, Sarah and I would be honored with your attendance.

Fondly,
James

THE WESTERN UNION TELEGRAPH COMPANY.
This company **TRANSMITS** and **DELIVERS** messages only
on conditions limiting its liability which have been assented to
by the sender of the following message.

Received at *Culpeper, Virginia* Date *April 23, 1867*
Sent from *New York City, NY*
Will arrive at 4:30 in the afternoon of April 24 at the Richmond train station.
Moses

Epilogue

1867

The minute I stepped off the train in Richmond, I spotted him. Though it had been thirteen years since we had last laid eyes on one another, I recognized him instantly. James was striding toward me, bearing the same confident posture that he always had...such rhythm to his steps, head held high, chin jutted slightly forward, and his shoulders tucked neatly to the back as if he were trying to make his shoulder blades touch each other. And that big wide grin! Such a contagious smile. I couldn't help myself. Without even thinking about it, I found myself beaming right back at him. His sandy, curly hair and fair complexion seemed exactly the same as I remembered.

Loping along next to James was a younger version, almost an exact likeness. When this youngster made eye contact with me, I couldn't help but think that his handsome, piercing blue eyes were so like those of Missus.

James and I approached each other swiftly, with extended hands, ready for a hearty handshake. Instead, we found ourselves embracing each other like the long-lost friends that we really were. With everything to say and yet nothing to say, there seemed an interminable quiet while each of us wrestled with the significance of our meeting again.

I don't know what was going through James' mind, but I sure

knew what was going through mine. In that short space of time, I relived many moments of those early days...a flashback of our shared history. As I struggled to rein in my emotions, James was the first to break the silence.

"Mother would be so pleased that you have made the long journey from New York to attend her funeral." James added, "She was always so fond of your family."

Still not able to put all of my thoughts into meaningful words, I simply replied, "James, she meant more to us than you can possibly guess, and I could not have let this time pass without my presence. I only wish that Mama, Addie and her husband, and my wife were here also. I am representing all of them. Please know that their hearts are with us now."

Trying to bring some levity to the serious moment, James said, "Moses, I haven't had a chance to tell you about this wonderful young boy next to me. Surely you have guessed by now that he is my son. No way could I deny that, the way he looks like a spitting image of me!"

"Moses Porter, let me introduce you to Moses Porter!"

With that, I let out a hoot and a holler! Goodness knows no end, James had named his son after me!

Both of us grabbed each other in another bear hug, thumping each other on the back and grinning like the cat that ate the canary.

Young Moses seemed convulsed with laughter when he said, "Are the tongues going to be wagging at Grandma's funeral!

We got a Negro Moses Porter and a white Moses Porter here for the funeral. Father, we always have been good at giving folks something to talk about…looks like that isn't about to change!"

Obviously enjoying that thought, James chuckled along with Moses and me, then noted, "We have so much catching up to do, but right now, Moses, let us help you with your baggage and get started on the short trip to our home. I am eager for you to meet the rest of my family. Sarah and her husband Connor arrive tomorrow morning."

Before we entered the church, I saw Cuffy, Lafayette and Lizzie and their daughter Rachel, now a teenager. I could not help myself. I ran to them and embraced my friends whom I had not seen for so long. Cuffy, looking quite old, gave me a bear hug and whispered in my ear that he had made Missus' beautiful casket, just as he had made Papa's. "It's more beautiful, Moses. I now have the luxury of working with fine tools and beautiful wood."

"Cuffy, what you did for Papa was also beautiful and I thank you for it," I said.

Lafayette and Lizzie looked so dignified in their somber black suits. They still looked like the calm, peace-loving people that I remembered. Rachel was now a beautiful young lady, but I remembered all the times I tickled her when she was a baby and she sat on my lap. I had to introduce myself to her. She did not remember me. I was still a young man, but seeing her so grown up made me feel old.

Missus' funeral was unlike Papa's. I understood that there are significant cultural differences, and I quietly observed and appreciated the distinctive ways whites and blacks celebrate the lives of their deceased loved ones.

There were beautiful flowers atop Missus' casket and in two flower stands on each side of the room. An organist played quiet music as the guests entered the room. Those attending the service were both black and white.

The minister opened the service with a short prayer.

Dear Lord,

We ask that you comfort us today as we honor Martha Eliza-beth Porter. Together we grieve our loss and give thanks that such an honorable woman lived among us. Life on this Earth is always uncertain and often too short. Be with us today as we share our love and our sweet memories.

Amen.

Following the hymn, *Abide with Me,* James stepped up to the pulpit to deliver the eulogy of his mother. His words were thoughtful and respectful as he described the grace with which she endured a difficult marriage and the practice of slavery, which she abhorred.

James shared details of Missus' life that were entirely new to me. She and her sister had enjoyed a loving, secure and happy childhood on a farm near Front Royal.

On a windy evening, their barn caught fire. Both parents ran into the barn to save the animals, opening the sturdy doors to the pasture and letting the horses out. Their father did not see his wife leave the barn and went back in to search for her, calling out her name at the same time that he instructed his daughters to remain right where they were - outside of the barn and safe.

That was the last time the sisters saw their parents.

"My mother's sister, Abigail, took over the responsibilities of the farm with significant help from friendly neighbors and relatives. Aunt Abigail has shared with me that Mother was extremely lonely. Aunt Abigail tried to bring some joy into the home, especially at holidays, but Mother was inconsolable.

"Along came my father, who seemed to be successful as a tobacco farmer. He lavished attention on her and promised that, with the birth of children, they would re-create the happiness she experienced as a child. How I wish that had been true," James continued.

"My beautiful and kind mother found herself living with an angry and dominating husband, who seemed unable to make her happy. She did find love in her children. Sarah and I adored her. She also found love and joy in the lives of the slave children who lived on our property. At a time when it was not acceptable to treat slaves as equals, our mother did. Some of the things she did with and for slaves would surprise most of you here today,"

James said, looking directly at me.

"Mother taught Sarah and me the many ways we should love one another. She influenced our lives in so many ways. I cannot imagine a world where she is not present."

Wiping a tear, James concluded, "Our children will miss her. Sarah and Connor and Charlotte and I will miss her. We will all miss her."

Filled with emotion, I knew that I, too, missed her. She changed our lives completely. Without her help, I am not at all sure that we would have found our freedom.

While James spoke, I wondered, *What happened to Mingo, Exeter, Hanson, and Flemming after they ran away the night that Ben left? What would my life be like now if Missus had not encouraged us to run away when she did? Would I have stayed on the plantation until slaves became free under the Emancipation Proclamation?*

I had some regrets. I regretted not being able to say good-bye to Paris, Lafayette and Lizzie, Rachel, and our other friends in the quarters. I regretted that I had not been with James and Sarah to comfort them when their mother was ill. I regretted that I never had the opportunity to thank Missus. Yes, that was my biggest regret. What a strong woman. She had the guts to do the right thing in spite of the times she lived in…in spite of the beliefs and feelings of her husband…and in spite of the risk she undertook. I wanted so badly to speak to her right then. *Missus, you will never know how your actions on that beautiful September day in 1852 changed our lives. We will never forget you. We will always love you.*

We walked from the church to the cemetery, following the horse-drawn hearse carrying Missus' coffin. At the graveyard, James read a prayer and Sarah led everyone in singing "Amazing Grace." Flowers were tossed onto the casket as it was lowered into the ground. I stood and walked toward the grave and placed my freedom stone among the beautiful roses atop the casket. Turning away, tears ran down my face, and I could not stop them. I finally allowed myself to cry - for Missus, of course, but also for Papa. For an end to slavery. For healing.

Judi Howe Bio

Passionate about the importance of reading for school success, Judi Howe started writing books for children in retirement. Her long career included being a middle and high school teacher, a business owner, and a published author of a sales training book.

Currently working on another middle grade novel, she lives in North Carolina with her husband of fifty-four years, and lives close to their daughters, sons-in-law, and five grandchildren.

Photographs and Illustrations

Chapter One: (Whipped slave with scars) Library of Congress Print and Photographs Division, Washington, DC 20540. #14043-2, no. 606. McPherson and Oliver, photographer, No known restrictions on publication.

Chapter Two: (The Big House) Library of Congress Print and Photographs Division, Washington, DC 20540. #HABS ALA 49-MOBI, 48-18. Considered to be in the public domain. No known restrictions on publication of images.

Chapter Three: (Slave boy with plow) Purchased stock image.

Chapter Four: (Missus' bedroom) Courtesy of Carolyn Merchant, PhD., Professor of Environmental History, Philosophy, and Ethics, University of California, Berkeley.

Chapter Five: (Slave quarters) Courtesy Carolyn Merchant, PhD., Professor of Environmental History, Philosophy, and Ethics, University of California, Berkeley.

Chapter Six: (Christmas Party) Purchased stock image.

Chapter Seven: (Slave funeral) Painting by John Antrobus, ca. 1860, held by Historical New Orleans Collection. Copyright has expired for all works published in the United States before 1923, now in the public domain.

Chapter Eight: (Harriet Tubman) Library of Congress Print and Photographs Division, Washington, DC 20540. Lindsey, Harvey B., photographer, (1842-1921). LC-DIG-ppmsca-54232. No known restrictions on publication of images. Published before 1923, in the public domain.

Chapter Nine: (Fugitive Slave Poster) Be Ready to Receive Them, Rauner Special Collections Library, Dartmouth University, Hanover, NH, 10/16/2012

Chapter Ten: (Uprooted Tree and Surrounding Thicket) Purchased stock image.

Chapter Eleven: (Frederick Douglass) National Portrait Gallery, Smithsonian Institution, Washington, DC. Unidentified photographer. 1856. This media file is in the public domain in the United States.

Chapter Twelve: (False bottom wagon) Courtesy of Mendenhall Homeplace of Historic Jamestown Society, Jamestown, NC.

Chapter Thirteen: (Small skiff with oars) Purchased photo from Turbo Squid.

Chapter Fourteen: (Steam train) Purchased stock image.

Chapter Fifteen: (Rough Waters) Purchased stock image.

CPSIA information can be obtained
at www.ICGtesting.com
Printed in the USA
FFHW02n1201131018
48757764-52835FF